The Ojanox

Lonesome Mountain

Daemon Manx

Published by Last Waltz Publishing

5 Midland Ave, Pompton Plains, N.J. 07444

All characters in this book are fictitious or used fictitiously with consent. Any resemblance to actual persons living or dead, is purely coincidental.

www.lastwaltzpublishing.com

Edited by Lisa Lee Tone

Original developmental edits by Ben Eads

Library of Congress Cataloging-in-Publication Data

Robert R. Chiossi, 1967-

The Ojanox Series / Daemon Manx

TXu 2-417-807 2024
ISBN 979-8-9909638-3-2

Book Cover by Christy Aldridge (Dark Poppy Designs)

Illustrations by Christy Aldridge and Don Noble

First edition October 2024

ALSO BY DAEMON MANX

Abigail

Piece by Piece

Drawn & Quartered with Diana Olney

Hacked in Two with James G. Carlson

These Lingering Shadows

Tales from the Monoverse

Arcranium with Mark Towse

Manx-iety: A Collection of Disturbing Stories

The Ojanox Series: I-IV

Scream in the Dark

Ashes to Ashes

All Fall Down

Lonesome Mountain

PRAISE FOR THE OJANOX

"In *The Ojanox*, Daemon Manx creates a community and cast of characters you feel like you know personally, like you've known them all your life. And when you lose one of those characters, you've lost one of your own. Manx makes you care and makes you hurt. *The Ojanox* is a masterclass on characterization." – Patrick C. Harrison III, Author of *Grandpappy* and *100% Match*

"*The Ojanox* harkens back to the horror boom of the '70s and '80s, in a very good way. Manx has a knack for creating characters you'll love (or hate) and putting them through the wringer. His dialogue is sharp and storytelling gripping and fast-paced. Now that I'm hooked, I need to read the rest!" – Duncan Ralston, Author of *Woom* and *Ghostland*

"Every so often, a writer reads a coming-of-age tale that they wish they had written themselves. That's how I felt with Daemon Manx's *The Ojanox* series. Exciting, genuinely nostalgic, and scarier than hell!" –Ronald Kelly, Author of *Fear, The Essential Sick Stuff,* and *Southern-Fried & Horrified*

"In Garrett Grove, the time for evil has arrived, and Manx serves up scares like Halloween candy—the good kind, too ... full-sized, nostalgic, and satisfying to the end."—Gaby Triana, author of *Moon Child*; editor of *Literally Dead: Tales of Halloween Hauntings*

"Daemon Manx has wrapped up a delicious candy treat that you won't be able to resist gobbling down, razor blades and all. *Scream in the Dark* will put you in the Halloween spirit no matter what time of year you read it. You'll be holding out your plastic jack-o-lanterns for more!" — Jeff Strand, author of *Twentieth Anniversary Screening*

"Daemon Manx has proven in a short time, he is the real deal. And he doesn't mess around. This is a must-read series, and one of the best books I've read this year." –Mike Ennenbach, author of *Cuckoo*

"If you are like me and love horror mixed with great storylines and twisted endings, you must read Daemon Manx. And when you are through, hug the pillow, hide under the covers, and repeat over again, it's only a novel ... or is it???"—Jason Knight - ECW Original

"Written with beautifully descriptive scenes, *The Ojanox* places you directly into the quaint, small town of Garrett Grove during the Halloween season where everything is pleasant ... until it isn't. An ancient, dark entity is accidently excavated and escapes into the world with chilling results. *The Ojanox* is a fresh, original, plot-driven page-turner that I couldn't put down. I highly recommend it and am looking forward to Part Two of this excellent series." – Jeani Rector, Editor of *The Horror Zine*

CONTENTS

In memory of Anthony Lorraine

Godspeed, my friend

FOREWORD

GAZING INTO THE ABYSS

The year is 1979. A small New York town prepares to welcome the fall season in all the expected ways: young children bicker and boast over Halloween costumes, secret lovers meet in clandestine corners, and a tortured soul plots wicked deeds. All the while, hidden just out of view, patient and hungry ... an ancient evil lurks.

I know, I know. You've heard all this before. You've read the book, watched the film adaptation, and probably even caught the two-part podcast. If you're a fan of old-school horror, like I am, then you'll swear that you know how the plot will unfold. What the primeval horror is. Who will live, who will die, and even in what specific order said deaths will occur.

Hey, I get it. I thought so too.

But I was wrong, dead wrong. You'll probably be wrong too. And, let me tell you, rarely has it felt SO good to be incorrect. To be legitimately surprised. To revisit a hallowed era of storytelling in such a creative way.

Let's be honest: vintage horror is a difficult thing to effectively pull off in today's market. Try too hard and you alienate your target audience, skewing far afield from that elusive "feel". Half-ass it and you're derivative, lazy, or a hefty combination of both.

For anyone who is familiar with his talent, Daemon Manx has, quite unsurprisingly, accomplished something special with *The Ojanox*, making the familiar feel wholly unfamiliar. Pulling us back to the gritty world of late-70s to early-80s horror without stepping on any toes in the process. This is neither an homage nor an emulation. This is a book that could very well have been borne of that halcyon era, resting on some half-askew bookshelf this whole time, just waiting to be discovered. But, as much as *The Ojanox* is a glimpse across decades, it is also a gateway into Manx's mind–one can glean various details about the novelist through the terrors nestled within the typeface.

Much like there are no atheists in foxholes, there are no innocents amongst horror authors. We write from the darkest of depths, from places where light falters and even whispers carry great weight. Yes, the stories we create are ultimately meant to startle, to shiver, and to scare. To invoke those primal sensations of fear and dread. But there is so much more to it than that. We are also, through prose and plot, offering the world a glimpse of our vulnerable sides. Our hopes and fears. The hardships we have endured. Mistakes we've made, and the fallout that followed. From pen to page, our pain is made manifest. Some people suffer for their creations–horror authors put themselves through anguish for their art. And, during this process of composition, this literary baring of souls, we allow ourselves to examine our personal hauntings, be they self-induced or inflicted by others. To exorcise our own demons, keystroke by keystroke. True, we may never completely vanquish the darkness inside us. For many horror authors, those hurts are grafted to our very essence, as much a part of us as blood and bone, woven into the very fabric of who we have become. But, while those shadows may yet linger, we at least get the chance to look our fiends in the eye with an unflinching gaze.

Daemon has never been shy about his personal struggles, of which he has had plenty. I respect both his candor and his fearlessness in facing those dark years. Perhaps that deep well of experience is what gives his writing that extra bit of compelling oomph. Some of us have pint-sized imps on our shoulders, gently reminding us of past indiscretions, tempting us back with honeyed words. Manx has a thousand-pound gorilla clinging to his back, beating its chest and bellowing a mighty roar of misdeeds, yanking at the chains of the past with inhuman strength.

And that, dear reader is what you get with *The Ojanox*. A beast of both the literal and figurative sense. A peek at the demons without ... and those within. This is a massive story, years in the making, touching on a myriad of topics, many of which are just as pertinent today as they were in '79. From a word count perspective (it shouldn't matter, but we're novelists ... it matters) it is an imposing body of work, rivaling the hefty behemoths of the era, as is only fitting. From my first involvement with *The Ojanox*, I have always maintained that Daemon writes like Laymon, but with a more literary bent. This isn't a knock at all: Laymon penned some classics. He was great at concepts, with a knack for the perverse and deft skill at setting a scene. The only place I was occasionally left wanting was with the narrative voice itself. Daemon rectifies that shortcoming with the ease of raw ability, wrangling words in the best of ways. In all honesty, it wouldn't shock me in the slightest to see Manx and Laymon sharing space on bookstore shelves in the not-so-distant future. I am hard pressed to think of an indie author who deserves it more.

But don't take my word for it. See for yourself. Curl up in your favorite space, dim the lights, crack open *The Ojanox*, and step into the town of Garrett Grove. What you find just might surprise you.

Jack Wells

Author of *Jack of All Trades* and the *Monochrome Noir* series.

Trick or Treat

I hope you will indulge me just a little before diving into the book, as the origination of *The Ojanox* is almost as interesting as the story itself. I began the writing process during the spring of 2020 while I was serving my final year of incarceration in a halfway house in Newark, New Jersey. Yes, you read that right. I spent nearly a decade in state prison prior to that. The short story: I made some terrible mistakes because of addiction (rarely are addicts known for making good ones), and that landed me in a very dark place.

But that was only the beginning of my journey because prison is where I finally got clean (Eleven years and four months as I write this today) and it's where I turned my life around. But something else happened while I was serving my days behind the wall. I started writing again. Addiction had stolen everything I loved, and my creative muse was only one of the casualties. But as the fog lifted, my desire to create returned, and it was in a cold, lonely cell where I started to live once again.

By the time I reached the halfway house, years later, I had written dozens of short stories and novellas but had never tackled any larger projects. It was January of 2020, and I had just received permission to leave the halfway house for a few hours a day to attend college in person. I even got a couple months under my belt, and then Covid hit. The house was put under quarantine lockdown, and no one was allowed to leave. Unfortunately, the virus had already found its way into the building.

And that was life for the next seven months. We started out with almost three hundred men in the facility, and that number quickly diminished to less than a hundred. We all got sick during that time, some more than others, and many of the men were taken back to the prison system's medical facilities ... never to return.

To pass the time, I started writing what I thought would be a short story, one that encapsulated the feeling and the mystery of Halloween the way I remembered it as a child. I sat down and wrote the first lines of what is now chapter one, and *The Ojanox* was born. Within a few days, I realized this was not going to be a short story. I had no idea just how massive it would be, but I was about to find out.

I owned a portable word processor called the Alpha Smart 3000, originally intended for my college classes. If you're not familiar, The AS3K is a battery-operated unit with a small screen that allows the user to see three lines of script at a time. There are eight files you can fill with text, but once they are filled, you must transfer the data to a Word doc and zip drive. I would fill the files every night, writing from 6p.m.–11p.m. non-stop. The next day I would use the house's library computer to transfer my work and ultimately free up space for another night of writing.

I should mention that I shared the room with ten other men who were anything but quiet. Who can blame them? We were all stir-crazy. While they were listening to music, playing poker, and screaming to one another in the confines of our 12 x 12 room, I would don my headphones, crank up the tunes, and write, write, write.

And yes, it was like that. I wrote in a fever; the words flowed as if they were coming from somewhere other than me. It was very stream of consciousness, but it was also methodical. During the day, I would map out the next ten scenes in outline, and that night, I would write. Oddly enough, not once did I experience even an ounce of writer's block.

On October 30, 2020, I typed the words *The End* and looked down at a massive file containing 520K words. I had finished the first draft in six months. Seven days later, I was released.

Now would come the hard part. The rewrite. Little did I know, I would be rewriting this beast for the next four years and editing out over 160K words, all for the betterment of the story, I assure you.

Now it's true that this story was created under some very adverse conditions. You could even say it is a byproduct of that suffering. But that's not why *The Ojanox* was written in such a short period of time. To be honest, I have been working on this story since I was ten years old myself. Like Troy Fischer, when I was in fourth grade, I had a Halloween party and built a haunted house in the garage. Yep, you guessed it, it was called Scream in the Dark. In *The Ojanox*, many of the settings, themes, and circumstances are inspired by my memories of Halloweens gone by and my own life experiences as well. However, this story isn't just a tribute to my own childhood but to childhood itself. If I have done this correctly, it is to pay respect to that initial sense of mystery we all felt when we heard our first ghost story, to that chilling fright when we saw our first horror movie.

Although the coming-of-age factor is just a small portion of this story, as *The Ojanox* is pure horror with its fair share of violence, I mention it because that's where it started for me ... when I was a child. My love for horror, that is.

If I got any of this right, I hope you are taken back, if only for a moment, to that innocent time in your life when you set out to grab a pillowcase full of candy on Halloween and returned home with all the peanut butter cups you were hoping for ... and more.

Daemon Manx

"Only then will you understand what has been delivered on the breeze. Only then will you know the beast by name. You say it with your dying breath ... Ojanox." ~ Lois Fischer

CHAPTER 87

Thursday

The Nor'easter that buffeted Garrett Grove and half the state of New York dumped a record ten inches of rain in just under five hours. The Lenape River swelled above its banks, flooding the low-lying areas of town and consuming what remained of the Gables Bridge. The damage from the heavy winds was extensive; from Route 3 to the top of Garrett Mountain, there wasn't a dwelling or business left untouched. Even the rockslide on Sunset Pass looked as if it could have been caused by the storm. On any other day, officials from Warren would have already come to check on their distant neighbors. But it wasn't any other day, and the storm had not been isolated to the Grove; Warren and the neighboring towns also experienced catastrophic damage. The power failure in Garrett Grove wasn't an anomalous occurrence either. Before the entire grid collapsed, a total of seven transformers had blown, sending an overload to the two step-down transformers at the substation, and a loss of one of the turbines. This resulted in an overload at the Con Ed Power Plant, which also effected the town of Warren, who had miles of downed lines and blown transformers of their own to deal with.

The rain had almost been enough to douse the numerous house fires that occurred throughout the town ... almost. Most were the result of extinguished pilot lights or overturned appliances as families were taken by surprise when hell smashed through their front doors and picture windows. Stoves were left on, fireplaces unattended, and candles had been knocked to the carpet. By the time the storm was over, most of the fires had burned themselves out.

An unearthly silence blanketed the streets of Garrett Grove. It spread out from the mountain like a tumor, silencing the usual chatter of wildlife in a suffocating shroud. The birds didn't call to the approaching dawn, nor did they ride the first thermal waves of the morning. Squirrels didn't scamper from branch to branch, and the chipmunks were nowhere to be seen. The larger animals were silent as well ... as if they'd never been there at all. And long before the first streaks of gold paved way for the rising sun, a deathly hush dominated a town that had once been alive.

The starkest contrast was the absence of people. Not one vehicle moved across a single stretch of pavement. The parking lot at Wilson's Diner was empty, as was the establishment itself. No coffee was prepared, no showers were turned on, and no early morning diapers were changed. Empty cribs sat in empty nurseries in empty houses on empty streets. It had been swift and impossible to stop, even for those who were aware of what was going on. The town had been infected by something far worse than anything Dr. Malcolm could have ever suspected. It had been ravaged by a plague. A plague that had silenced countless species in the past. And though it had been known by many names, they all meant the same thing ... extinction.

The surviving members of Ted Lutchen's group spent the night in the back room of the pharmacy at the medical center. The gauntlet they'd set up at the nurses' station had been ineffective; they were overrun and forced to retreat to the stairwell and then onto the roof, where they made their final stand. With the beasts closing in, Ted considered the unthinkable: using his weapon to spare his friends and then turning it on himself. But before he could act on the thought, it was over, the creatures ceasing their attack and disappearing into the storm. But there had been casualties, a great number of them. Alice and Will Tobin, Ed Koloski and Grady Martin, Nurse Carole, not to mention every living soul that sought shelter in the basement. However, they found little carnage when they made their way from the roof through the third-floor hallway where the battle took place. There was a tremendous amount of blood and gore but nothing that could be identified. The creatures had assimilated or consumed what remained of the patients and fallen members of Ted's party, as well as countless numbers of their own. A fortunate Billy Tobin had been spared from finding the corpses of his entire family.

Ted kept watch throughout the night while the others rested. Even after what they had been through, they had all managed to fall asleep. Everyone except for Billy, who sat across from Ted, unblinking. The kid had lost everyone. Ted couldn't fathom how the guy was still functioning, how he hadn't broken down. The way he had chased after Dawn onto the roof without concern for his own safety surprised even Ted. The guy was a warrior. *Billy the Kid,* Ted thought as he inventoried the ammunition and weapons they had retrieved from the hallway.

Doris and Burt rested in one corner of the cramped area, while Dawn, Cyndi, and Baxter huddled together in another. All was quiet except for the occasional snores and chuffs from the coroner and the dog, then about an hour before sunrise, Ted rose to stretch his legs.

"I'll be right back," he told Billy, the only one awake.

"Are you sure it's safe?"

Ted shrugged. There was no way of knowing. The creatures had abandoned their attack when they could have easily finished the job. It was possible some had remained to scavenge the detritus of the dead, but Ted didn't think it likely. He would take a quick tour of the hallway, then make a pit stop in the men's room; his bladder had been screaming for over an hour.

He left the back room of the pharmacy with Billy locking the door behind him, then made his way through the second-floor hallway. All was quiet; the red glow of the emergency lights revealed nothing out of place. Ted kept his revolver in hand and proceeded with caution. He turned the corner, entered the men's room, and relieved himself. Standing at the sink, he stared at the unrecognizable face in the mirror. The dim light accentuated the bags under his eyes and reminded Ted of pictures he had seen of his old man. He splashed himself with cold water and was drinking down several mouthfuls when a blast of static squelched from the radio on his hip. He seized it and shouted into the mic.

"Come in. Is there someone there?"

"Thank God." The sheriff's voice was followed by another blast of static. "Good to hear your voice, Ted. What's your status?"

Ted didn't want to say too much for fear of Lois or the children overhearing. He had no idea how to share the news about those they had lost and figured delicately was the best approach.

Carl appeared to anticipate what Ted was thinking and cut in before the deputy could continue. "I'm alone. You can speak freely."

Ted took a deep breath. "Not everyone made it, Sheriff. The only ones left are Burt and Nurse TenHove, Billy Tobin, a candy striper named Cyndi, the dog, and the little girl." Ted stared at the strange face in the mirror and added, "I'm sorry."

There was a long pause before the sheriff replied. "Copy that. Tell Doris and Burt I will be there shortly after sunrise. I have a child with a massive head injury that requires immediate attention. Meet us in the emergency room and tell them to be ready. The kid's hanging on, but I don't think she's got much fight left in her."

"Roger that, Sheriff. We'll be ready when you get here." Ted ended the transmission and turned the water back on. He watched it form a funnel as it ran clockwise down the drain and tried to remember why it did that. *Why always clockwise?* His overtired mind was unable to recall what he had learned in school, how the metallic particles in the water were affected by the earth's magnetic poles. Not that it mattered. He splashed water on his face and prayed they might survive the day. Ted made his way back to his group, then led them through the abandoned medical facility to the emergency room.

They arrived on the first floor, and the group went straight to work. Doris and Burt prepared for their patient, and Ted sent Billy and Cyndi to the cafeteria to drum up something for breakfast. Dawn and Baxter remained behind, never straying from Ted's side.

"Deputy," Doris said. "I need you to contact the group at the high school. Find out if Dr. Freedman and Michelle Marks are available. Tell them their presence is required immediately."

Ted acknowledged and headed for the exit door. The sun had just begun to turn the color of the sky into a pale shade of pink.

"This is Deputy Lutchen to Bob Jones. Come in." Ted hadn't heard any of yesterday's transmissions and knew nothing of their status. He waited for a response that never came, then tried again. He knew it was impossible to transmit through the school's concrete foundation, but the dead silence led him to suspect a different explanation. He didn't know if Doris and Burt could handle what was coming their way but hoped their combined talents would be enough to save the child. A disturbing premonition gripped him, and Ted doubted if any of Garrett Grove's doctors had survived the night.

Carl was up before the sun and ventured out of the armory just as Ted was leaving the pharmacy. The basement of the sheriff's station revealed no sign of the menacing threat; it appeared the beasts had vacated the building sometime in the night. He cleared each room with his service revolver in hand, then made his way upstairs. Satisfied the place was secure, he contacted Ted, and although he hadn't had time to express himself, he was happy to hear his deputy's voice. But Carl was running on fumes; he couldn't remember a time he had been so thoroughly exhausted in his life, not even in Vietnam. Sure, he had been tired during the war, both physically and emotionally, but he was younger then and able to endure the sleepless nights.

Now it felt like he had been buried under a landslide, and the lack of sleep was only part of it. What affected Carl to his core was the insurmountable loss and despair that swept through his town like the angel of death. Something he said a lifetime ago came to mind: *People don't get murdered in Garrett Grove—not in my town.* He rubbed his temples, trying to force the cobwebs out of his head. He had kept Lois and Troy alive by sheer luck. If they were going to survive another day, it would take a lot more than that; he needed to stay sharp.

He tore through the supply closet, found what he was looking for, and returned to the basement. The group regarded him through bloodshot eyes when he entered the armory carrying the wooden stretcher. Wendy and Troy huddled near Janis, who had started to moan and managed a few incoherent words in her unconscious state. Carl maneuvered into the room unsure how he would break the news to Lois about Will and her sister, and knew now wasn't the time. It would be awful when he finally did, but he needed everyone as clear-headed as possible. Transporting Janis to the medical center would be difficult enough.

"The building is clear," he said. "The sun will be up in a few minutes, and I think it's safe to move Janis." Wendy and Troy met his stare. "She needs medical attention, and we'll use the stretcher to carry her." He knew the best thing he could do for the children was include them, so he assigned each of them a task and then set the stretcher beside the cot with Lois's help.

Even in the dim light of the armory, the deep purple bruise that crept across the girl's face was prominent. It flowed out from under the bandage like a stain. With the children off gathering supplies, Carl, Lois, and Jessica transferred Janis onto the stretcher, then carried her to the back of the mayor's station wagon. They grabbed everything they possibly could, knowing there was a good chance they would never return, then the group left the building.

Carl drove while Lois and Jessica did their best to secure the stretcher. Troy and Wendy sat in the backseat staring out the windows at the destruction. The spot where the two cruisers collided was the first scene of carnage they encountered. Both vehicles had burned throughout the night; all that remained were the hulking shells. When they turned left onto the Turnpike, the enormity of the devastation became apparent. A vehicle had crashed through the front window of the Plains Pharmacy; a splattering of crimson gore decorated the display shelves in a haphazard frenzy, making it look as if the owners had started to repaint the place in the dark.

The front of Bell's Hardware looked like it had been hit with a wrecking ball. Carl swerved around a Volkswagen Beetle overturned in the center of the road; a horrible dark brown stain spread out from the smashed-in windshield. Other vehicles had been left abandoned in the street as if they had run out of gas or just stopped working. The once familiar neighborhood was now a post-war scene of desolation; the absence of life was ubiquitous. Not so much as a squirrel darted from behind a single branch; the trees themselves looked as if they had witnessed something beyond unspeakable.

Houses had caught fire, many burned to their foundations. No one had been called to battle the blazes; even if they had, there had been more pressing matters than a few pieces of burning timbers.

The rain had moved on, but the wind was still strong in the wake of the storm. A cluster of papers blew across the street, and Carl knew what they were before the bills caught in the wagon's windshield wipers. The faces of Franklin and Grant stared in at the passengers as the vehicle lumbered past the Herald Bank. The front doors were destroyed; thousands of dollars now littered the parking lot and the street. Carl doubted the creatures had done that. Whoever thought the present catastrophe was a good diversion to hit the bank had either overestimated their own limitations or underestimated the nature of the catastrophe.

Carl checked the rearview to find Troy and Wendy wide-eyed with wrist rockets held at the ready.

He rounded the corner near the high school and drove straight to the entrance of the medical center. He pulled into the lot and made his way to the emergency room entrance to find Billy Tobin waiting at the door. Carl looked back at Lois, who hadn't yet seen her nephew, and prepared himself. *Son of a bitch!* He knew things were about to get even worse. He felt horrible for not having told her about Will and Alice; he had spared her a few moments of sorrow but doubted it would matter.

Ted exited the door and helped Carl with the stretcher. As they rushed into the building, Lois screamed and then started crying; her short reprieve was over. Her sobs permeated the building, echoing off every surface. A moment later, Troy's tears mixed with his mother's.

Doris directed the men where to place the stretcher. She and Burt were dressed in scrubs and had an array of equipment and supplies laid out on trays next to the bed. They transferred Janis to the bed and then began to examine her wounds. A low, almost inaudible gasp escaped from Doris's throat, but she quickly recovered and went to work. The nurse filled a needle from a bottle that said epinephrine and inserted it into the girl's arm.

"Gentlemen," she said to Carl and Ted. "I need you to remove yourselves from the area. We're working under adverse conditions and must take every precaution to prevent infection."

The men took several steps back when Burt approached and locked eyes with the sheriff. Carl nodded to his friend; the old man's voice resonated in his head as if he had spoken aloud. *This isn't going to end well, even if she does manage to survive.* Burt pulled the curtain and returned his attention to the patient.

Doris cut away the gauze and removed the bandages. "Oh Lord," she gasped, looking down on the wound. The child's hair was caked with dry blood, but Doris could still make out the ruinous indentation in the girl's head. The entire left side of Janis's face had bruised and swelled under the pressure of the concussion.

Together, they began to clean the wound, with Burt handing off items as Doris asked for them. The bed linens beneath the child began to turn red as the disinfectant washed the gore away. Doris had seen numerous head wounds during her time in the ER; concussions, even under the best circumstances, were difficult to predict as the brain swelled and pressed against the broken skull. Most were survivable, provided the damage wasn't too severe and the patient received prompt medical attention. But Janis had been unconscious for over twelve hours, and judging from the color of her face and the amount of blood loss, Doris believed the blood vessels in her brain had been compromised. At the very least, there had been some extent of brain damage. It was a miracle she had survived the night.

"Peanuts ..." The word escaped from Janis's lips, followed by a low moan.

Doris and Burt stared at one another, wondering how the child was still able to speak. The girl was a fighter. Burt made the sign of the cross and said a prayer. Janis moaned again and then muttered something that sounded like "you bacca," but neither were able to understand what she was trying to say. Then the corners of her mouth turned up as if she were trying to smile. She spoke again, and this time they were able to make out every word.

“Troy ... be careful.”

Carl motioned for Ted to follow him, then led the deputy to the remains of the lobby. The entire front of the building had been smashed inward as if it were hit by a tank. Broken glass and twisted metal littered the floor, and a thick smearing of black tar trailed to the buckled basement door. Carl sensed the apprehension in his young deputy, who couldn’t stop staring at the stairwell.

“I won’t ask you to go down there,” Carl said. “Not yet. You’re sure no one survived?”

“I don’t see how anyone could have,” Ted replied. “I have no idea how we made it ourselves; it was the damnedest thing. They had us surrounded on the roof, we were outnumbered, then they just vanished.”

“I need to get over to the high school. It went bad there too.” Carl removed his hat and untucked his shirt, which was covered with Janis’s blood. “That thing that got into Rainey’s head ... it happened again, or it never left in the first place. He showed up at the high school last night with a fucking arsenal and killed damn near everyone. Andrea had to put him down. This thing used our own man against us. How do you protect against something that can do that?”

“Jesus, Sheriff.” Ted’s face went pale.

“We need to find a way to get everyone out of town before nightfall. I have no idea how we’re going to do that. The pass and the bridge are out, and the river will be impossible to cross with the children and seniors.” He unbuttoned his uniform and threw it to the side; the T-shirt underneath had a small smear of blood but nothing by comparison. It wouldn’t comfort anyone if he showed up at the high school bathed in gore.

"I need you here, Ted. So far, they've only attacked in the dark, but stay sharp. While I'm gone, I want you to figure out an escape plan. I don't think we have another night left in us."

The sheriff exited out the broken front doors, and Ted returned to the emergency room to find Burt and Doris still behind the curtain, focused on their patient. There was no sign of the other members of his group. He left the area and headed to the cafeteria. Minutes later, he walked in to find everyone seated at one of the larger tables with Cyndi and the mayor busy behind a gas grill, flipping pancakes. The aroma of frying bacon and melting butter hit him like a freight train, causing his stomach to lurch in response. A stronger scent cut through the others and made his mouth water. Someone had brewed coffee, and it smelled intoxicating.

He approached the table where the small group of survivors gathered and offered his condolences. Ted Lutchen was no stranger to loss, though it had been years since he experienced it firsthand. Having spent his early years in different foster homes and then losing his adoptive parents when he was young, he knew there was little he could say that would help. He had been on his own ever since and considered himself lucky that he didn't have anyone left to lose, or so he thought.

CHAPTER 88

Bob Jones and the survivors at the high school spent the night huddled together in the back room, far away from the carnage in the main area. A group of just over three dozen mulled over a breakfast that had been prepared by several of the firemen; it did little to placate the grieving. Kelly Rainey clung to Jill Boriello like a baby kangaroo to its mother's pouch. Jerry Santos, Ralph Walsh, and a handful of the other children gathered around Miss Davis; none had left her side, not even to use the restroom. Tyler Harrison and Rich Marek assisted the seniors and helped feed them breakfast. The Bentley family stayed to themselves, trying their best to avoid the accusing stares from those who had not been as fortunate. It had been sheer luck that spared the Bentleys from the madman's bullets. But this morning, no one wanted to hear a damn thing about luck, so Günter and his brood sat away from the others, in the far corner eating cold cereal.

When breakfast was finished, Bob pulled Brandon to the side and led him out of the room. "You're with me. Do you have your weapon?"

Brandon showed him his sidearm, then followed the chief through the main area, past the rows of covered bodies. Bob unlocked the door to the staircase, and the men ascended. Neither had any idea what they might find in the gym or in the parking lot, but they couldn't stay in the basement; it had become a morgue.

They entered the gym to find it empty and quickly made their way to the exit doors. Bob pressed his ear to the steel and was alerted by the sound of approaching footfalls in the parking lot. He pulled back the hammer on his revolver and aimed at the center of the door.

"Hello. Is anyone there?" a familiar voice called out. "It's Sheriff Primrose."

Bob let out a sigh of relief and holstered his weapon. He motioned for Brandon to do the same, but the boy shook his head in response.

"How do we know it's really him?" Brandon asked. "It could be one of them like Rainey."

The kid had a point; they had been blindsided by an enemy that knew their weaknesses. Bob raised his weapon again and yelled through the door. "I'm here, Carl. But how do I know it's really you?"

There was a moment of silence, making Bob think the kid had been right, then Carl answered. "Good thinking. I guess there isn't much I could do to prove it without you seeing me. You probably have your guns drawn, so I'm removing my weapon and placing it on the ground. Of course, you can't see that, but when you open the door, I will keep my hands on my head. You can take my gun until you're convinced that it's me."

"Okay," he yelled. "Back away from the door."

Bob removed the chain securing the door, pushed it open, and raised his weapon; Brandon followed his lead. Carl smiled with his hands glued to the back of his head and stood there when the men emerged from the building and retrieved his weapon.

"Is it really you, Carl?" Bob squinted against the harsh morning sunlight.

"In the flesh," he said, making no sudden movement.

"Christ, it's good to see you." Bob holstered his weapon and looked at Brandon to do the same. "Put that damn thing away before you accidentally kill someone." He seized Carl in a bear hug and knocked the wind out of him.

"It's good to see you too, old friend," Carl replied, hugging him back.

Bob released him and looked down at the blood smear on the shoulder of Carl's T-shirt. "Where's your uniform?"

"We were in an accident ... One of the children." He paused. "We had to hold up in the armory until it was safe to leave. Doris and Burt are doing everything they can. Please tell me Dr. Freedman made it?"

Bob shook his head and met Carl's stare; he didn't need to answer but continued. "Michelle Marks is alive; she could assist Nurse TenHove."

Carl let out a thousand-pound sigh as they entered the gym and made their way toward the stairs. "I want you men to put your heads together," he said to both Bob and Brandon. "We have to get everyone out of town before sunset, and I need answers on how we are going to do that."

Bob shook his head and smiled.

"Tell me you have an idea."

"Not me, but I was talking to someone who does. I think it would be best to let him explain it to you, and a good idea to get everyone out of the basement." Bob's voice shook as they started down the stairwell. "It's awful down there, Carl ... It's just awful."

"I wish I had time to be a bit more sensitive to what you've all been through." Every eye zeroed in on Carl as he addressed the survivors in the back room of the shelter. "Unfortunately, time is of the essence, and right now, the important thing is getting you out of this basement and to safety. We're headed to the medical center to regroup with the others. The emergency generator is supplying minimal power, and there's hot water and plenty of beds. We're working on an evacuation plan, so as soon as you are ready—"

The promise of a hot shower got everyone on their feet and moving faster than even Carl expected. No one wanted to spend another minute trapped underground with hundreds of bodies just a stone's throw away. They gathered their limited belongings and made a mass exodus past the acre of corpses. Carl approached Andrea Geary, who was one of the last to leave the room. The glazed look in her eyes told him she was beyond shell-shocked; she had been defeated.

"He killed them, Sheriff. I didn't have a choice." Her voice lifted as if it had risen from a grave.

"I'm sorry." Carl stopped her and put his hands on her shoulders, causing Andrea to tense up. He hadn't been positive but had reason to suspect that she and Joel Kovach were romantically involved, cop intuition or maybe just his gut. "I can't imagine what you're going through. They were my men, and I loved them too; Joel was like a brother to me. And Rainey ... I swear, Andrea, we're going to get out of this; I just need you to be strong a little bit longer." Carl searched for the right thing to say, not wanting to sound cold or inappropriate. Something in his words appeared to affect Andrea, who looked up at him, a bit more clear-eyed, and forced a smile.

"Yes, Sheriff. I can do that." She left the room and headed upstairs just as Bob Jones approached with the Bentley family at his side.

"Carl," he said. "I believe Mr. Bentley has an idea you will find quite interesting."

"I'm looking forward to hearing everything you have to say, Mr. Bentley. Perhaps you could share it with me on our way to the medical center. You can all accompany me in my cruiser."

"Zat vould be goot, Herr Sheriff," Günter replied as he and his family followed the sheriff and the chief out of the basement and into the light of day.

On the way to the medical center, Günter explained his idea to Carl. It was a damn good one, and Carl couldn't believe he hadn't thought of it himself. Of course, it would have been impossible to execute yesterday due to the storm. Also, the plan couldn't accommodate a large group; however, their numbers had been greatly decreased. Carl followed the school bus to the center and listened to the supermarket manager lay out his plan in detail. And for the first time in a very long week, Carl Primrose felt hopeful. *This just might work.* It would have to; they were out of options.

CHAPTER 89

As the sun began to rise, Don and Stephanie stood at the mouth of the cave, staring out at the stillness of the quarry. The storm had passed, and from what they could see, there was no sign of the creatures that had descended from the mountain. They gathered all they could carry, taking several of the ancient tubes and anything that resembled a lodestone weapon, and made a break for Don's truck.

The horror of what happened to Garrett Grove was quickly revealed the moment they turned onto the Boulevard. The town was unrecognizable. Vehicles lay in tangled wrecks, abandoned, and overturned; some had been driven into storefronts, and others had been ripped apart. Numerous fires had occurred. Some of the homes and businesses were still smoldering, while others had burned to the ground. Telephone poles and trees had fallen, blocking the road with debris and downed power lines, forcing them to backtrack and find alternate routes.

A deep, guttural gasp escaped from Stephanie's throat when they turned into the Village. Don swerved at the very last second to avoid driving over the body lying in the center of the road. It was impossible to tell if it had been a man or a woman; there was little left that was identifiable. The poor soul's intestines trailed out from the remains as if they had been used for a game of jump rope; dark brown blood saturated the pavement.

Other houses had fallen in Stephanie's neighborhood. Windows were smashed in, front doors torn off their hinges, and many had caught fire. There were more corpses littering the development as well, lying on the front lawns and trapped in their vehicles; none appeared to be intact. Stephanie pointed to the Cape Cod on the left and burst into tears as Don pulled into the driveway. The house across the street was gone. A scattering of debris blanketed the front yard; the splinters that had been someone's home still smoldered.

"No!" Stephanie screamed and was out the door and running before Don came to a full stop.

There were no other cars in the driveway, and the front door had been smashed inward. Don watched Stephanie bound up the steps and disappear into the house. He quickly followed, finding pieces of the shattered jamb laying on the soaking wet carpet of the entranceway.

"Janis! Lynn!" Stephanie screamed from the back room. Don knew she was wasting her time; it was obvious the place was empty. She sprinted past him in a flurry and ascended the stairs three at a time. She called out and ran from one bedroom to the next, searching for her sister and daughter. The sound of her heavy footsteps echoed like thunder throughout the tiny house. Finally, she stopped moving as if she had found something.

"What the hell were you doing with this?" she said. A moment later, she raced down the stairs toward Don with what looked like a photo album tucked under her arm. She hurried out the front door without stopping. "They're not here. Let's go!"

They arrived at Don's house minutes later to find the place in even worse condition. Not only had the front door been smashed in a similar fashion, but the back door was broken as well. The bodies of countless creatures littered the entrance way and the first-floor rec room. A fight had taken place; by the looks of it, the creatures hadn't come out on top. All the monstrosities looked deformed, as if they were missing a few chromosomes. One of them resembled a reptile of some type, possibly a snake. Others looked more like a cross between human and primate.

Don walked through the rec room trying to piece together what might have happened. He approached the table he used for his prints and picked up the cardboard box. "Look at this," he said, turning it over so Stephanie could see.

The front of the box read *Devlin's Assorted Magnets*; the contents had been removed and the package left on the table. Don scanned the room and noticed the open toolbox in the corner, not the way he had left it. Then he saw the hammer and chisel laying amidst a litter of small black chips. He knelt, picked up the chisel, and watched as several of the chips attached themselves to the tool. He pulled off one of the magnets and showed it to Stephanie, who nodded and tilted her head to the side.

"Here," she said, taking the book from under her arm. She opened it and turned through the pages. "I think our children were looking at this. I couldn't understand what would possess Janis to go in my room and dig it out ... until now." She showed Don the page that the book had been opened to when she found it on her daughter's bed; it was titled *Cahokia* and contained several black and white photographs. The pictures were of weapons similar to the ones they had found in the cave; musket ball-sized spheres, arrowheads, daggers, and spear tips—all appeared to have been fashioned out of lodestone.

"Are you saying our kids knew what the hell was going on and figured out how to fight it?" Don looked down at the broken magnet in his hand.

"It looks that way," she said. Scanning the room, Stephanie spotted something near the back window and walked over to retrieve it. "Look!" She picked up the jagged shard of magnet and showed it to Don. The pointed angles gave the object the appearance of a sharpened projectile. The kids had used the hammer and chisel to smash the magnets into the perfect-sized weapons.

Don rifled through the empty bag left on his drawing table and fished out a receipt. "Magnets and three wrist rockets. Son of a bitch!"

"They were here." Tears brimmed heavy in the corner of Stephanie's eyes and ran onto her cheeks.

"Do you think our children did this? Is that even possible?" Don said, taking a moment to study the creatures and their wounds.

"I don't think a wrist rocket could do that kind of damage," she said. "Some look like bullet holes."

Don nodded in agreement. The damage appeared to have been caused by a large-caliber bullet. Which meant the children had held their ground until help arrived. One thing was certain, the kids had figured out what was going on long before anyone else had. And knowledge was the key ingredient to survival.

Together, he and Stephanie searched the rest of the house, but there was nothing else to be found. They were returning to the driveway when Don spotted another body in the backyard near the garage. A shiver settled into his spine, and a cramp gripped his heart in a stranglehold; something about the way it lay near the open door. He ran toward the corpse without saying a word, and Stephanie followed.

The primitive creature lay on its back with three small puncture wounds in its chest. A dark liquid oozed from the beast, matting its hair and staining the tatters of its remaining clothes. Don removed a ballpoint pen from his pocket and inserted it into one of the creature's puncture wounds.

"What are you doing?" Stephanie asked.

"I just want to see something," he said, tapping the pen into the damaged flesh until it connected with something hard. He twisted the pen and pried at the object. It popped out of the wound and landed in the grass between his feet. Don touched the back of the pen to the small black shard and watched it jump out of the grass and attach itself to the metal.

"It's a magnet." He held it up for Stephanie to see.

Her jaw fell, then she turned toward the open garage door behind them and motioned toward it. They entered the building to find two more bodies and the place torn apart. "So, this is Scream in the Dark," she said, examining what remained of the haunted house.

"What's left of it. I'd say your little girl finally saw it. They got out of here in one piece; I'm sure of it. We just need to find out where they went from here." Don remembered hearing the air raid siren but couldn't recall where any of the town's shelters were located. The only place he could think of might be the sheriff's station and figured that was as good a place as any to head to next.

He turned to exit the garage, stepping over the torn down cardboard pieces and remnants of what was left of Scream in the Dark. He approached Stephanie, who stood with her back to him, facing the same wall where a young Robert Boyle had stood just five days before. He reached out and touched her shoulder, immediately sensing the tremors ripping through her body.

"Hey, we're going to find them," he said.

Stephanie faced him, her eyes red and swollen and tears streaming down her cheeks. The tremble of her bottom lip caused her teeth to chatter. "I have a terrible feeling." She allowed Don to wrap his arms around her and draw her close.

"Don't talk like that."

"I can't help but think this is all my fault."

"You couldn't know any of this would happen. No one could."

"No." She pulled back and looked at him. "For what I did ... for what we did. I-I'm not religious, but as far as karma goes, I messed up big-time. What if this is karma. Oh, God—if something happened to any of the children, I'll never forgive myself."

CHAPTER 90

The overall mood at Our Lady of the Mountain was exuberant for almost everyone except Father Kieran. Any general would consider the results of the previous night's battle a victory, but the loss of even one member of his flock was unacceptable. Allison was the first to arrive at the church, and she had been his sign from God. Her death was a significant sign as well, and her passing was devastating. More than ever, Father Kieran felt the reignited fire in his belly to bring the battle to the enemy. He wanted to hit them where it hurt, and thanks to Allison, he knew exactly where to strike. Allison had provided the strategic information and become a martyr in the process; now she was the inspirational force driving Kieran's determination to rain holy hell on the evil one.

The beasts attacked and then fled like cowards after realizing the parish was too great a force to overcome. Kieran's army kept a vigilant watch throughout the night, but the creatures never returned. When the sun rose on a new day, the newly formed militia prepared a victory meal fit for the

Knights Templar. They used the rectory's gas stove to prepare the food and served breakfast in the parking lot.

Kieran knew the odds were in his favor and their best chance for a swift maneuver was to attack while the demons slept. After the meal was finished, the congregation cleaned and reloaded their weapons, packed their supplies into the vehicles, and formed a convoy leading to the top of Mountain Ave.

They filled the parking lot at Mountainside Park and left their vehicles on either side of the street. Then Father Kieran addressed his flock, offered a prayer to the Lord, and they began their arduous ascent up the abandoned Old Mountain Ave extension. The group assaulted the gate separating them from the treacherous road; rather than navigating a safe passage around it, they tore it down and trampled over it.

The old road didn't look any better in the early morning sunlight than it had the day a thousand snakes cascaded down its crumbled asphalt and attacked the Tobin brothers. It was still just as cracked and forgotten, although there were no reptiles to be found. There were no birds either, or squirrels, or chipmunks, or anything else one would expect to see in the early morning hours on Garrett Mountain. The road was silent; the only sound was the marching feet of Kieran's army.

The frenzy of the impending fight seized the crowd like a drug. It made their skin tingle with anticipation, set their nerves on fire, and filled them with a super-heightened sense of awareness, as if their morning coffee had been spiked with amphetamine.

There was one member of the flock who still wasn't buying all the gung-ho dogma the priest was selling. Amy Sterling didn't feel half as optimistic and had attempted to voice her concerns at breakfast. But she had been cut off and silenced by members of a cult that had been recruited less than twenty-four hours ago.

The loose gravel made traveling hazardous, and Amy had nearly fallen twice already. With every step that brought them closer to their destination, she became more certain she wanted no part of it. Still, she followed the others, kept her mouth shut, and waited for the right moment. She ascended the steep incline until she came to a spot where a large branch sat amidst a cluster of loose asphalt, and decided to make her move. Amy stepped onto the scattering of pebbles and allowed her foot to slip out from underneath her. She came down hard, more on her fanny than anything else, grabbed her leg, and screamed.

"Ahhh!" she cried. "My ankle." Amy grabbed her wounded foot and rocked back and forth on the loose pavement. Julie Evans rushed to her side.

"Are you all right?" Julie asked.

"I think so." Amy tried to stand but fell again when she transferred her weight.

Julie helped steady her friend while the rest of the congregation gathered around them. Father Kieran parted the crowd and knelt beside the girls. "Are you hurt badly, my child?"

"I think she sprained her ankle, Father," Julie said. Amy looked up at the priest with a tear in her eye.

"I'm afraid you won't be joining us in battle, Amy," he said. "I'm sorry."

"I can make it, Father." She tightened her face in pain.

"I'm sorry, but we can't take you." He placed his hand on her shoulder. "We will come back for you after we defeat the beasts." Kieran motioned to Dick and Josh. "Brothers, help Amy to a comfortable spot on the side of the road. Our sister has fallen." He turned and addressed the crowd. "It is here where we must part ways ... let us march!"

Dick and Josh grabbed Amy under each arm and assisted her to the side of the road. They sat her down on a patch of grass in the shade, checked to see she was comfortable, then joined Father Kieran and the rest.

Amy wiped away the tears that had come naturally, not the ones she intended to shed to sell her act. She took Julie's hand, pulled the girl close, and whispered in her ear. "Don't go up there. Please stay with me."

"I can't." Julie's eyes welled up. "Luke." Her husband had bought into what the preacher was selling, and there would be no talking him out of going. "My place is at his side ... for better or worse. I'm sorry."

"You can't." Amy tried to hold on to Julie as the girl pulled away.

"I'll come back for you." Julie turned and joined the rest of the group.

No ... no you won't. Amy wanted to scream and beg her friend to stay with her but knew there wasn't a thing she could say that would change her mind. Instead, she watched the congregation continue up the steep road until they disappeared over the crest. She removed a pack of cigarettes from her coat pocket, lit one up, and let the smoke swirl around her head on the cool October breeze. Her plan hadn't worked out quite the way she intended; she had hoped Father Kieran would have dispatched a member to stay behind with her, Julie preferably. But the priest was committed to the fight, and the thought hadn't crossed his mind. He was blinded by his own bloodlust, and Amy was the only one who had seen that. Julie knew it too but refused to leave her husband's side. *Fools.*

Amy stood up and flicked her butt into a loose patch of asphalt where another girl had fallen less than a week ago. That girl was also dead. Amy brushed the dust off her jeans and started to walk down the old, forgotten stretch of pavement, being extra careful to watch her step. The last thing she needed to do was fall and twist an ankle.

The front doors of the sanatorium had been left open, the hinges now rusted and frozen in place. Most of the windows in the building had been broken by drunken teenagers along with every mirror and interior pane of glass. Father Kieran held the large-caliber pistol in his hand and stood before the oppressive structure for the first time, the perfect sanctum for the Dark One. The grounds reeked of suffering and despondency; every pore of every brick cried out against the horrors that endured for years behind its now decaying walls. The looming monolith cast a dark shadow across the battered asphalt. Standing before the desperate structure made the priest's head swim and his eyes water. Father Kieran tried to ignore the sour pit in his stomach as it turned like a screw being threaded too tightly. He bit back against an overwhelming sense of intimidation and forced a smile, then he rallied his troops one last time before ordering them forward.

"The Lord is with us today," he said, standing tall in the shadow of the sanatorium. "Stay sharp and we will be triumphant! The beast sleeps by day; we have the element of surprise on our side. We will dispatch the demons and end their suffering. And they will be thankful that we did." Father Kieran ascended the front steps of the sanatorium and entered the building. His entire flock followed without a word of resistance.

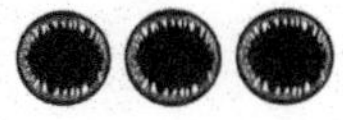

For decades, Mountainside Sanatorium housed members of society who required isolation to prevent them from infecting the rest of the population. Now a far deadlier infection resided in the old hospital, one that made tuberculosis look like a case of the sniffles. This one possessed a consciousness, and it knew the minute Kieran and his flock entered its home. It had been waiting for them, after all ... and they were welcome. It had been a long time since the old hospital had visitors, even longer since the Entity had devoured a group so sure of themselves, so confident they had the upper hand. But the one called Allison had revealed their plans, and it was prepared. It had relocated the three that possessed its essence, separating them from the brood. Although it had little concern for the priest and his soldiers, the bodies of the little ones were weak and would soon need to be replaced with fresh hosts. There was no reason to risk unnecessary exposure when it could easily dispatch the priest's forces from where it now slept, miles away in the minds of Rob, Erin, and Ben.

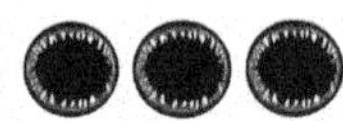

Sometime between Tuesday morning and Wednesday night, Angelo and Donna Franco had come to believe in monsters, leading to a quick restoration of their faith. Although it hadn't been lacking to begin with, during times of desperation, there was always a fire sale on the product. And the young couple had bought what Father Kieran was selling ... in bulk. Even Donna, who had been paralyzed with fear only a few days ago and unable to walk across her neighbor's kitchen floor, now found herself filled with a sense of invincibility. The young couple were the last to climb the crumbling stairs and enter the foyer of the building. The overpowering funk of mold, decay, and death permeated the place like a vapor. It hit Donna in the face, causing her to gag as the putrid stench filled her mouth and sinuses. She doubled over and retched, then noticed the stains on the moldy tile floor. An army of oily black tracks covered every inch of the tile; most of them looked fresh.

Donna jumped at the jarring concussion of heavy metal slamming behind her. Although she knew she'd been the last to enter the building, she turned back toward the entrance expecting to find someone had shut the doors behind them. But no one was there ... no one had slammed the front doors ... because the doors were no longer there. The stairs, the entrance way, and the foyer she had passed through only seconds ago were all gone. A solid monochromatic ocean of dark red wavered before her. The crimson hue of the wall reminded Donna of the dried blood left on her neighbor's kitchen floor.

She spun about, reached for Angelo's hand, and came up with nothing. Her husband, who had been standing at her side, had been replaced by another wall of scarlet identical to the first.

"Angelo!" she screamed, spinning three-sixty to locate her husband and the other members of the party. Everyone had disappeared. Donna found herself surrounded by the repulsively-colored surfaces. The ceiling and floor had also been transformed into the solid shade of drying blood, making it impossible to discern where one flat surface ended and the other began. There were no visible right angles; the monotonous flow of the landscape made Donna's head swim. She swayed on her feet, overcome by a dizzying sense of vertigo. Finding it impossible to attain depth perception from the flood of sensory input, she reached out to grab on to anything that might help steady her. She took a lumbering step forward, then another. Donna's hands smacked against something wet and were sucked in up to her elbows.

She screamed and struggled to pull her arms free from the suction of the wall, but it held fast and began to pull back. Donna jerked with a violent twist and managed to yank herself free; she was slapped across the face by the warm wet liquid. It was rancid and smelled much like the stench that had hit her when she first entered the building, only far more concentrated. Examining her hands to see what had splashed her caused Donna's heart to stifle in her chest. Her arms were covered in crimson from elbows to her fingertips, dripping thick with deep red blood. Her eyes struggled to focus on the coating; it appeared to be pulsating on her skin. Then she felt it ... it was moving.

Donna looked closer to find thousands of tiny red worms clinging to her flesh. They flipped and twisted along the entire length of both arms. She twitched when the first one crawled across her face and over her eyelid. Donna reacted and brushed it away but only managed to transfer more of the small creatures onto her cheek.

She screamed and began swatting at the worms, then tried to scrape them off her arms, which only aggravated them. The first one bit into the skin just above her wedding ring, followed by another that nipped her on the wrist. As if they had been waiting for a signal, the entire swarm of maggots bit into Donna's flesh on cue. Hot white light erupted behind her eyes, and every pain receptor in her brain fired as the worms burrowed into her flesh. They ate at her, digging away tiny channels into her skin and biting her face. Donna's head flailed as if in the grip of a grand mal seizure. All the while, her hands clawed to remove the worms that simply were not there.

The suggestion planted in her head had been small but effective. It took root and snowballed, her neural network doing most of the work itself.

There was an inaudible snap as the thin thread connecting Donna to reality was severed. She bucked and twisted, then hunched over and started running at top speed. Her fingernails tore deep gouges into her forearms as she attempted to scratch the worms out of her flesh. Lost in a sea of scarlet, Donna struggled to outrun insanity. But it already had control of the reins, propelling her forward with no idea she was in motion. She ran across the lobby toward the thick marble banister of the staircase with her head lowered like a battering ram. Her feet skated across a scattering of loose plaster, but somehow, she remained upright, and she continued to build up speed.

Donna's head connected with the unforgiving solid marble. The sickening crunch that her spine made when it snapped at the brainstem was audible, but it was only heard by her; she had simply mistaken it for the sound of a worm biting into the soft flesh on her neck. And Donna Franco was dead before her body hit the floor.

Not far away, a dark presence found great satisfaction in her death; it had almost been as satisfying as if it had consumed the woman itself… almost.

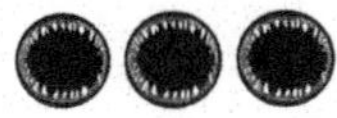

Just as Donna turned to find herself face to face with the scarlet apparition, her husband, Angelo, was thrust into a nightmare of his own. The lobby stretched out before him as if the walls, floor, and ceiling were no more tangible than the exterior of a balloon. The expanse of the room elongated, walls that had been near twenty feet in length doubled, then quadrupled in size until Angelo could no longer see where they ended. The ceiling disappeared into an infinite void. His stomach flipped, and Angelo doubled over and vomited onto the floor, but that, too, vanished as the tile beneath his feet expanded into nothingness.

He stumbled for a moment, then turned to search for his missing wife. His eyes struggled to focus on the enormity of the endless hallway but found the task impossible to accomplish. Angelo raised his gun and pointed it down the hall; he thought about firing off a round, then hesitated. The hallway grew darker, and there was movement in the far distance.

He squinted at what looked like thermal waves and something suspended above the floor.

"Hello," he shouted. "Where is everyone?" Angelo began to make his way down the endless corridor. The .357 in his hand trembled, and the pulse of a bass drum beating against the back of his eyes made it impossible to see straight.

The void beneath him listed hard to the left, then pitched to the right. Angelo was thrown against one hard surface and then ricocheted into another. He managed to stay on his feet, but the gun was knocked out of his hand; he watched it tumble away down the hall. Angelo scrambled after the weapon and crouched to pick it up, but the gun was torn from his reach as if it were on a conveyer belt. With a jolt, the entire hallway heaved like the deck of a wooden ship caught in a hurricane, tossing both Angelo and the gun. He was thrown over five feet into the air, then came down hard on his side on top of the gun.

Angelo's shoulder popped out of the socket when the force of his downward momentum was halted by the unforgiving cold steel. The sensation of his extremity tearing out of the cup blinded him, and Angelo vomited once again. Searing pain like soldering irons probing his flesh brought him to the edge of unconsciousness, then pulled him back slowly. After what felt like an hour, he rose to his feet, his left arm hanging limp a good nine inches longer than the right. He winced against the pain assaulting his entire left side, picked up the weapon, and froze.

Angelo found himself in the middle of the movement he had seen in the distance. Icy breath escaped his mouth, forming long plumes of condensation in the frigid air. Huge slabs of meat, much bigger than any sides of beef Angelo had ever seen, swung back and forth, suspended from massive hooks connected to rusted chains. The encompassing stench of rot filled the air, and the only sound was that of a thousand flies as they feasted on the carcasses of spoiled flesh. The ceaseless rocking of the meat accompanied by the nauseating stench was nearly as maddening as the din of the insects as they rippled across the putrid grey flesh.

Angelo navigated a path around the slabs, being careful not to touch the meat or the flies. But the insects appeared to sense his presence, their droning song changing in pitch and timbre as he passed. All the while, the decaying carcasses swayed closer toward him as he turned sideways to clear a passage up the middle. Then he saw them ... figures coming toward him, lumbering down the hall from the opposite end.

He couldn't tell what they were but could see they were dressed in white and moved in frantic jerking motions. Sweat broke out on his forehead despite how cold it had gotten. There were two of them, much closer than they had been only a second before. They looked almost human but didn't move like any human Angelo had ever seen. Throwing their arms in the air, then bringing them down in violent sweeps, they ran at him with the intention of a freight train. Then he saw the butcher's aprons they wore and the cleavers they wielded. The fast-approaching menaces raised their weapons high into the air and then brought them down like lumberjacks against the rotting carcasses. Huge chunks of meat fell from the bones, sending swarms of flies into the air.

Angelo's lungs cramped as if they had shriveled in his chest at the ghastly sight. The creatures were featureless, devoid of any facial characteristics; they had no mouth, and no nose or eyes. But somehow their aim was deathly accurate. He froze where he stood, allowing the monsters enough time to hone in on him. Their blank canvas faces pointed in his direction, and they came at him like a tsunami. Angelo raised the gun and fired at the beast closest to him. The bullet hit it in the chest, causing the white fabric of its apron to run deep red. The second one reacted and bolted at

Angelo, who turned his weapon and fired. The lunatic butcher was felled by a bullet to the forehead.

Fighting to catch his breath, Angelo regained a small amount of his composure and raced down the hall, away from the rotting meat. He stepped over the bodies he had shot. Luke Evans and Diane Nathan had both been fighting their own individual nightmares. Neither had been wearing white or carrying a clever, but Angelo's bullets had worked on them just the same.

"Angelo, where are you?" Donna's voice called to him from somewhere down the hall.

"I'm here," he shouted. "I'm coming." He passed the last slab of hanging meat as fast as his throbbing shoulder would allow. The floor continued to pitch and toss him off balance, but Donna was nowhere in sight and Angelo was rapidly approaching the end of the hall.

"Angelo!" Donna screamed. "Hurry!"

Picking up the pace, Angelo pushed through the pain with his arm stabbing at him like a molten dagger. His feet landed on black-stained tiles as he approached the ancient elevator shaft that had been pried open a decade ago by a group of drunken teenagers. Donna's voice called up from the darkness of the shaft before him. Angelo was unaware of the Entity's presence.

He stepped off of the hallway floor and onto nothing. The feeling of weightlessness never registered as his other foot followed him into the darkness. In a heartbeat, he was falling. For a fleeting moment, Angelo realized something had gone very wrong. His body cartwheeled as it fell thirty feet down the abandoned shaft toward the mangled hardware that lay rusted and corroded at the bottom.

Angelo's body smacked against the hardened steel, and just like that ... the pain in his shoulder was gone. His spine severed in three places, and his skull cracked open like a cantaloupe filled with strawberry jam.

It watched the man's body shatter against the machinery. If it had working vocal cords, it would have been laughing, but the three children had lost that faculty some time ago.

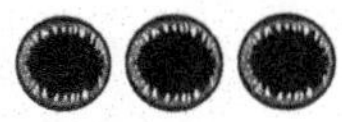

Julie Evans stepped out of reality and walked into a page straight out of Robert Boyle's notebook, which had been created and perfected in the mind of Troy Fischer. The Entity that consumed Robert was so enthralled by the idea of the ambush it couldn't resist utilizing the psychological manipulation.

Julie found herself thrust into absolute darkness, unlike the Francos, who had been consumed by visual illusion. A blanket of night closed in and suffocated her as if she was being held under water. Not even a shadow of black on black permeated the stark canvas devoid of sensory input. She reached out for anything to help navigate her way through the abyss, her fingertips tingling as they contacted nothing. A profound emptiness filled her, and fear lashed out as Julie made the quick progression from tears to sobs to hysterical panic. Her hand smacked against the wall to her right, allowing her to gain her balance, at least for a moment. When something brushed up against her left side, Julie screamed. She relaxed a second later, realizing it was the wall on the opposite side; somehow the hallway had grown impossibly narrow and closed in on her.

Julie soon found herself sandwiched between walls on either side, with just enough room to shuffle forward by turning her body sideways.

The darkness was overpowering. She sidestepped through the narrow corridor with one wall pressed snug against her back and the other tightly against her stomach and chest. She raised her arms alongside her without a thought for the firm grip on the pistol in her hand. Her ragged breath escalated; the frantic cries burnt like cinders in her chest. She forced herself to continue forward, but the hallway had grown so narrow she was unable to progress. She had come the wrong way and hadn't even realized it. Julie prepared to move in the other direction when it hit her. It blasted her in the face—hot, wet, and pungent—and Julie was acutely aware. Something stood mere inches before her and had just exhaled directly into her face.

Blinding white light erupted from every angle, searing her eyes and momentarily paralyzing her. It had happened so sudden and intensely that Julie suffered a minor heart attack on the spot. However, it wasn't enough to kill her, and the terror that followed shocked her back into the moment. The strobe flashed at a frenzied pace, revealing the cage she had pressed herself up against. The horrible beasts that occupied the space in front of her threw themselves at the bars and clawed at her. Covered in hair, their deformed faces contorted as they howled, filling the tight area with their noxious breath.

With no way to turn, she tried to sidestep in the opposite direction but found the act impossible. The walls closed in tighter around her as she struggled to move. One of the beasts smashed its grotesque face against the bars and shrieked, spraying spittle into Julie's eyes and mouth. She screamed and fought to free herself, her pulse thrumming in time to the strobe.

Julie's heart slammed against the walls of her ribcage and flooded her brain with too much blood. She stumbled over her feet and tried to force her way down the hall. She tensed up and squeezed the trigger of the weapon in her hand. Julie's arms had been raised in the confines of the hallway, and the bullet didn't have very far to travel. The hot lead slammed into her temple and bounced around inside her skull, tossing the grey matter like a Caesar salad. Her lights went out, and she fell to the floor between the bodies of her husband and Diana Nathan. Troy Fischer had been correct about the effectiveness of his idea; in the end, Julie Evans really did Scream in the Dark.

Jimmy Reilly flanked Father Kieran up the stairs of the old hospital and was the second man to enter the building. But the moment he cleared the threshold, he fell victim to the same mind trap as everyone else. The Dark One had left a present for the priest and his followers, one that would ensure the safety of the Entity's children while they slept in the basement.

Jimmy found himself walking through the halls of Garrett Grove High School. He knew he was late for his next class and raced down the hall to the boys' room. He passed one of the classrooms and caught a glimpse of his boyish features in the glass. His youthful face had still been intact back then, and Jimmy was beginning to forget it had ever been otherwise. The crowd of students that progressed the halls appeared to separate as he made his way forward, as if they sensed his presence and didn't wish to impede his momentum. He raced to the restroom with an overwhelming urgency to relieve himself, then turned the corner into the pungent surroundings. He entered the stall and unzipped his fly, feeling he might just piss himself. He smelled the sulfur and saw the cherry bomb sitting in the toilet a second before it exploded. The bowl shattered, throwing up tiny blades of shrapnel at him. Jimmy had enough time to close his eyes before he felt the first shard penetrate his cheek.

Jimmy made his way down the hallway; the memory of the past few seconds faded as he tried to figure out where he was. Late for class ... that was it. Somehow, he had gotten tied up, and he was about to miss the final bell. Worse than that, he had to piss like a goddamn racehorse. He double-timed it toward the boys' room and caught a glimpse of himself in the window of one of the classroom doors. He smiled when he saw himself; he always liked the face the Lord had blessed him with and couldn't wait for his confidence to catch up with the rest of him. He imagined he would become quite the ladies' man one day. He ran into the bathroom, barged into the first stall, and unzipped his fly. The world was eclipsed in a deafening concussion and blinding light. The pain in his face exploded like he had fallen onto a fire ant mound, the razor-sharp pieces of porcelain making quick work of his flesh.

The crowded hallway of the high school was nearly impossible for Jimmy to navigate. He was already late, and on top of that, he had to go like there was no tomorrow; if he didn't make it to the bathroom soon, he would surely piss himself, which he hadn't done since kindergarten. His bladder screamed but not as loud as the pain he felt in his face and his head. He passed one of the classrooms and turned to look in the glass as he walked by. The face that stared back at him was unrecognizable; it was horribly disfigured, as if it had been in a terrible accident years ago, and never healed correctly. Jimmy tried to force the image out of his head, thinking it had been a trick of the light or his own mind playing games with him. He rounded the corner and entered the bathroom in a frenzy with his belt undone and zipper halfway down. He ran into the stall and began to piss; he had been holding it for so long.

Before he could react, there were hands on him as someone grabbed him from behind and pushed him forward. It was Butchie Post, the school lunatic; the guy had had it out for him all year. Jimmy struggled but was unable to move while Butchie held him and pulled his pants to the floor. "Hold still, pussy!" Butchie screamed, pressing up against him.

Jimmy struggled to get away from the madman, but every move he made allowed Butchie a better hold on him. *What the hell is he trying to do?* Then he felt it press up against him as the monster forced his head into the toilet. His face submerged under the water as the lunatic pressed harder against his backside and invaded him. *Dear God, what's happening*? It was the last thing he thought before the bomb exploded and took half his head off with it.

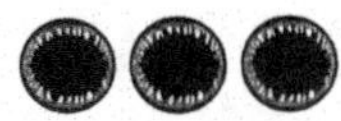

Jimmy stumbled through the empty hallway of the high school, tripping over his own feet. Blood flowed down the front of his shirt and splattered onto the floor. His pants hung around his ankles as he shuffled off in a direction he had no idea he was heading. Bells rang in his head, making it impossible to think or even focus. He almost fell when he entered the bathroom but managed to hold on to the wall for support. Jimmy made his way to the sink, then stood before the mirror. Half of his face was missing; his left eye hung out of the socket, suspended by a mass of veins and optic nerves. His stomach somersaulted at the sight of the beast in the mirror that looked an awful lot like him. Before he could fully react, he was grabbed from behind and manhandled to the floor, unable to understand what was happening with the two percent of his brain that still worked.

"Hold still, pussy!" a familiar voice said, the owner shoving something stiff into Jimmy's ass. He lay there as the creature forced him to relive the scene over and over until Jimmy's brain was as limp as an overcooked piece of spaghetti.

Jimmy Reilly moaned on the lobby floor of the old hospital with drool running from his mouth in a steady stream; he pissed himself repeatedly.

The Entity ransacked what was let of Jimmy's frail psyche and destroyed it in less than three minutes.

Chapter 91

Father Kieran had underestimated the enemy; even worse, he had overestimated himself. He had mistaken the creature for something as simple as a demon or a fallen angel. He was unaware of the intelligence it was capable of, nor could he fathom the measure of its hunger for domination. The priest's deceptive victory the night before had been a ruse to extract information and lull Kieran into a false sense of security; and the priest had fallen for it like a child.

The intel obtained by the portion of the Entity residing in the misshapen body of Erin Richards was all the tactical advantage needed to thwart the priest's forces at the gate. It ransacked Allison's simple mind and assimilated her into the brood. Her addition proved helpful when it came to laying the mind trap at the entrance of the nest. The enemy had simply walked into it; everything in their heads was there for the taking and easily used against them. The priest had taken down the one called Malcolm, and for that, he would suffer ... for a long time, for eternity if his mind allowed it. It had already tasted the man through the thoughts of Allison, and when the priest entered the lair, it knew all it needed to manipulate the man completely.

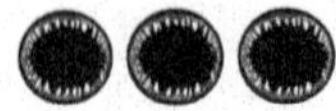

Sergeant Kieran McCabe ducked at the sound of artillery fire echoing in the distance. A mortar exploded a half klick from his position; the concussion was great enough to cause his ears to pop. He looked through the thicket of jungle to the other men in his platoon and motioned for them to stay down. The AK-47 he held tight to his chest was comforting yet thrilled him at the same time. He had killed more Viet Cong with the weapon than he could count and was about to add a few more to the list. He raised his hand and ordered his men to follow. He had been bred for leadership, and although he should have ranked higher than sergeant by now, he was glad he hadn't. It allowed him to fight alongside his men, as opposed to being stationed so far away from the action that the only fighting he would see was if he refused to pay one of the whores in Saigon.

He led the men through the brush and emerged first into the clearing on the other side. A cluster of commies gathered around one of the rat holes, preparing to go underground. He held up his fist, telling his men to hold tight, and removed the sidearm from his holster. The large .45 was a beauty and had one hell of a kick, also it left an exit wound the size of a grapefruit. He backed slightly into the brush and aimed at the first target. He preferred to use the .45; it was so much more personal, and he wanted to remember the kill.

Kieran fired at the man. The image froze like a Polaroid as the bullet entered the commie's forehead and exited out the back of his skull in a volcanic spew. He trained the weapon on the next man, who didn't have time to move, and fired again. Another bullseye; the man fell next to his dispatched comrade.

"This one's for Uncle Sam, you commie fuck!" Kieran hissed, squeezing off the final round at the last man as he attempted to enter the tunnel. The projectile caught him in the throat but failed to kill him; a river of crimson exited the wound in a deluge. Kieran rushed toward the man, stood over him, and pointed his .45 at the gook's head. Then ... the scenery shifted; the jungle swam into a blur of green and black, and vanished. Kieran looked down as the stained floor of the sanatorium faded into view.

He found himself standing over Dick Wilson with his weapon pointed at the diner owner's head. The man had been shot in the throat. He stared up at Kieran with terror in his eyes and scrambled to get away from the priest.

Kieran looked at the weapon in his grip; it was still smoking and hot from having been fired. *What have I done?* He scanned the floor of the old hospital and saw the bodies of the others where they had fallen. Bill Hamilton, the fire inspector, had been shot in the head and lay a few feet from the body of Frank Palumbo, the owner of the Texaco station.

Father Kieran knew it had been his bullets that took the men down ... but how? "Lord, how could you let this happen?" he demanded as Dick Wilson let out an asphyxiating gasp and collapsed on his back. The man had come to Kieran looking for salvation, hoping to find someone who might lead him in the fight against evil. The priest studied the smoking gun in his hand and started to cry. He had no recollection of drawing his weapon in the first place.

Other bodies littered the floor of the lobby; Kieran's tears fell and pooled with their spilled blood. Then he noticed the rest, the ones that were still alive, who stood there frozen in place. Josh Wilson had stopped a few feet from the main entrance; his jaw hung slack with his eyes rolled back in his skull, revealing only the whites. Others stood just as catatonic with their arms limp at their sides; many had dropped their weapons. One of the women lay before the banister; her head had been smashed in from an obscene amount of force. Kieran opened his mouth to alert the others. They had been ambushed and were being picked off one by one.

Then ...

Sergeant Kieran McCabe ducked at the sound of artillery fire echoing in the distance. He reloaded his side arm and waited for the exact moment to strike. He had always been destined to serve in the military and was determined to leave this war a hero, even if meant he would have to kill every last commie bastard himself. Which was exactly what he intended to do.

It played with the priest and forced the man to destroy the rest of his flock, just like a good little toy soldier. When the Entity had finally gotten bored with the man, it tossed him down the elevator shaft, where he landed next to the other creature. Neither body would go to waste and would provide some well-appreciated nourishment for its brood when they woke. The same was true for the bodies on the floor of the lobby.

It had expended a great deal of energy with the execution of the mind trap and retreated fully into the minds of the three. It rested and attempted to regain its strength. There was much that needed to be done before it moved into Warren. It needed to acquire the others, and then it needed to transfer.

CHAPTER 92

The small group ate breakfast in the wake of a most somber silence. The pancakes and coffee that Cyndi and the mayor served helped to alleviate a glimmer of the sting but did nothing to placate the wounds. They were all processing the loss in their own way, and it was something they would be dealing with the rest of their lives, however long that turned out to be. So many had died—best friends, neighbors, brothers and sisters, mothers and fathers. Despair had taken residence in Garrett Grove and knocked on everyone's door.

Billy and Lois, who were reeling from the deaths of Alice, Will, and Eric, did their best to offer Wendy and Troy their bravest faces. The children were in shock after all that had transpired in the past twenty-four hours. Having been attacked by the creatures, witnessing the destruction of the town, and the accident that had left Janis fighting for her life, it was a wonder they were able to eat at all. There were others who were still missing too. Don, Stephanie, and Wendy's mother hadn't shown up to either the high school or the medical center. It was possible they had all found a safe place to hide, although with each passing moment, that possibility became more unlikely.

While the others were internalizing their pain, Billy Tobin was redirecting his and projecting. More than anything, he wanted revenge. For some reason, he had been spared while so many others had not. Thanks to Father Kieran, he had been given a second chance to make it right. Billy wondered if the man had survived the night. His memory of the past few days was still a bit foggy, but the details were coming back a little at a time. An image of the priest standing over him came to mind, followed by a vision of a thousand serpents descending the face of the old road extension. He remembered looking up at the crest of the hill and seeing Butchie Post with his arms stretched out to the heavens, like he was controlling the snakes, like they were protecting something. *Son of a bitch!* The realization smacked Billy in the face. He had known what to do a week ago but hadn't been prepared. But he was weaker now and was in no shape to lead an attack himself. He scanned the room and surveyed their limited forces; there were so few of them left. They needed more manpower; they needed an army and someone who knew their way around a battlefield. *That's what we need. We need a seasoned vet.*

The cafeteria door flew inward, and Sheriff Primrose entered, followed by Bob Jones and a small group of people. Many were seniors and children and not exactly what Billy had in mind, but there were more than a few strong men among the ranks. Billy watched the sheriff direct the crowd into the cafeteria, and it all made sense. Somehow, he had known; even years ago when he had buried the man's car keys in the snow and thought it the funniest thing, he had known.

Wendy raised her head when the doors opened and the crowd poured into the cafeteria. Her eyes grew wide with anticipation, hoping the next face she would see might be her mother's. But as the line of new arrivals thinned, it became obvious her mother was not among them. Wendy sank back in her chair and attempted to stifle her tears.

Lois was about to try to comfort the girl when Troy leaned over, put his arm around Wendy, and hugged her. Wendy leaned against his shoulder, returned the embrace, and wept into Troy's shirt. Lois got caught in mid-breath and felt the air swell in her throat. She covered her mouth with a trembling hand and tried to hide her reaction. It was the single most profound gesture she had ever seen. It was as if the children had grown up overnight. Troy and Wendy looked more like a couple who had been married for years, perfectly in tune with one another's emotions, and not a couple of ten-year-olds who had just experienced their first kiss. It also struck Lois as far more genuine than even her own marriage. She wondered what might become of this puppy love that had blossomed under the pressure cooker of desperation. Troy kissed Wendy on the forehead, and it was too much for Lois to bear. The tears broke through her defenses and overflowed the banks. It should have made her worry about Don, but at the moment, he was the furthest thing from her mind.

Carl waited for the last of the new arrivals to be seated and approached the area near the front of the room, where he had addressed a much larger crowd only yesterday. He turned his hat over in his hands, searching for the appropriate words to begin.

"I'm not gonna sugarcoat it. There aren't many of us left and our options are limited." This was met with a grumble of concerns, and Carl knew he hadn't chosen the best opener. "But I've been talking with Mr. Bentley, and he has an idea that just might work. Günter is the instructor for the sailing club. He has informed me that there are three boats tucked away in the rec center at King Lake." Another murmur spread throughout the room; however, the mood had shifted some.

Most people in town knew Günter oversaw the club that met Saturday mornings to teach young boys and girls how to sail. King Lake was massive. It fed into the reservoir and supplied all the drinking water to not only the Grove but most of King County. Since it was part of the watershed, the only boats allowed on the lake were sailboats; motorboats were prohibited, as runoff from the engines polluted the drinking water. There were some fishermen in town who braved the lake in rowboats, but that was foolish since King Lake produced waves large enough to capsize the small vessels and had done so in the past. The sailing club owned three twenty-five-foot sloops, which was a bit of a luxury for the small community. They had been donated in the mid-sixties by a relatively famous mystery author who had retired to the Grove and later caught the sailing bug.

"There are three boats. To the best of my knowledge, they're the only ones in town sturdy enough to make the trip. Each boat can safely hold ten passengers." There was movement as everyone in the crowd started counting heads. Carl cut in. "You're doing the math right now. And yes, it will take two trips. It will also be dark before any of the boats return with help to pick up the rest of us. So, we're sending the women and children first; if there is any room left, we will do it the old-fashioned way." Carl held up his battered Stetson for all to see. "We'll pick names out of a hat.

I've chosen pilots for the boats. Günter and Hazel Bentley will be in one, Deputy Geary and Fireman Leone will be in the second, and the third will be piloted by Fireman Marek and Mr. Harrison. With a little luck, the wind will be in our favor and the boats will return before sunset." Carl turned to Günter, who offered a questionable look, then checked his watch. "It's almost ten. Mr. Bentley and my men are going to prepare the boats, which gives everyone an hour or so to get something to eat and wash up. Anyone who would like to assist the crew, please see Mr. Bentley or Deputy Geary."

There was a stirring at one of the back tables where a group of seniors from Botany Village had gathered and were in deep discussion. "Tell him ... tell him," the others urged one of the women, who turned and raised her hand.

"Yes." Carl recognized the former town librarian who had helped him with his book reports when he was a boy. "Yes, what is it, Mrs. Harris?"

"Well, Sheriff." She lowered her arm. "My friends and I have been talking, and while we might be old, we can still do math. You don't have enough room on your boats for half the people here." Carl nodded his head and opened his mouth to speak. "Let me finish before you cut me off, young man. You can kindly keep all our names out of your hat. If there's room on the second trip, that's fine, but make sure you get everyone else out before you worry about us. We've lived our lives, raised our kids, and spent more than our fair share of seasons in Garrett Grove. And to be honest, some of us old-timers won't be around in another year anyway. That's our decision, and we won't hear anything different. Thank you."

Carl wasn't the only one taken aback by what Mrs. Harris had said. No one had been prepared for it. Conversations erupted, mixed with astonished gasps and more than a few tears. Carl swallowed back the lump in his throat, offered a smile, and averted his eyes. "Well ... I suggest the rest of you take advantage of the accommodations in the meantime."

The crowd in the cafeteria began to disperse, but Carl remained at the front of the room to go over the details with Günter and his men.

Ted excused himself from the table, leaving Cyndi and Mayor Marceau to watch over Dawn and her dog, and joined Sheriff Primrose and the others. Although he arrived in the middle of the conversation, it was easy to get the gist of what was being said.

"Dat's not possible, Sheriff," Günter said. "Dere ist no vay ve vill be back in time."

"I know." Carl nodded and lowered his voice so that no one outside the immediate circle could overhear. He motioned for Andrea, Ted, Günter, and Bob to lean in close to him. "Under no circumstances are you to come back for the rest of us. There's enough room on those boats for all the children and most of the women, and that's going to have to be good enough. When you get to Butler, notify the authorities and call the National Guard, let them deal with it. That's an order."

"Sheriff." Andrea was again on the verge of tears. "You can't be serious. You just told everyone we would come back."

"I know what I said, but I couldn't risk creating any more of a panic than we're already dealing with. If anybody starts asking questions, just play along and tell them what they need to hear."

Andrea wiped the corner of her eye and nodded in agreement. Then Günter leaned in even closer with his lips pressed tight together. "I am not very goot at lying, Sheriff."

"Then don't, Mr. Bentley. But surely you can remain silent. If a question comes up that you can't answer, then just excuse yourself and tend to the boat ... weigh anchor, trim the sails. I don't know, do whatever it is you do on a sailboat." Carl offered the man the best smile he had left, which appeared to be just enough. Then he turned to the others. "Bob, Ted, I want you to help make sure that everyone gets on the bus by eleven thirty. The boats leave at noon."

The place was buzzing with activity; some helped themselves to what the cafeteria had to offer in the way of a meal, while others headed off to freshen up. Carl looked to where Lois and the rest of her group remained seated. They had not started to move, but soon they would have no choice. Whether she liked it or not, Lois and the children were getting on one of those boats, along with Mayor Marceau and the candy striper. The dog would have to stay behind, which Carl knew would present a problem, and then there was Billy Tobin. The kid had already been through hell and was one of the few family members Lois had left. He wasn't sure how he would do it, but when it came time to pick names out of the hat, Carl was going to make sure that Billy Tobin's would be the first.

"You have your orders." Carl raised his voice to its usual timbre. "Take your team and get those boats seaworthy, Mr. Bentley. Then call us on the radio when you're ready."

Günter nodded as Andrea closed the distance between her and the sheriff and wrapped her arms around him. She pulled him close and held on tight. "Be careful, Carl." She placed a kiss on his stubbled cheek and released him.

Before he could react, she turned and left the room. It was the first time she had ever hugged him or called him by name. Bob and Ted also sped off to do as instructed, leaving Carl alone for a moment. He replaced his hat and approached the table where Lois and the others sat. They looked up at him as he stood there searching for the words to say. Before he could open his mouth, Lois cut in.

"You warned me," she said blankly.

"What?" She had caught him off guard.

"You told me to leave two days ago. But I just couldn't believe it."

"You did what you thought was right. I don't blame you; I've been second-guessing every move I make. If it's anyone's fault, it's mine."

"That's not true, Sheriff," Billy said with a voice as stiff as iron. "I knew something was wrong last week. I should have come to you, but I wanted to take care of it myself."

Troy perked his head up along with everyone else seated at the table. They listened as Billy worked through what had happened to him nearly a week ago.

"It attacked us at the old sanatorium last Saturday night. We went there after Troy's party, me, Mick, Eric, and the girls. There was something up there. It looked like smoke, or maybe a cloud ... it was hard to tell. At first, it was behind us, but then we got freaked out and started running, and the next thing we knew ... it was in front of us. Damn thing flew over our heads like a flock of birds or something. Whatever it was, it was hunting us. Mick decided to lure it into the woods so the rest of us could get away. When he got back to the car, he was bleeding, said he ran into a branch, but that's not what happened."

Carl didn't want to push but was anxious for the boy to continue. "What else, son?"

"Sunday afternoon, Eric and I decided to go back." Billy cleared his throat and wiped his eyes. "It was my idea. I forced him to go. We picked Mick up; he had this rash on his neck, worst case of poison oak I ever seen. Only it wasn't any ordinary rash. We started to walk up the old extension to the top of the mountain ... then—" He paused, trying to force the memories to the surface. "I'm not really sure what happened, but there were snakes ... a lot of them, and that guy Butchie Post was there."

Carl felt his stomach churn at the mention of the name; that was one headache he didn't need to deal with at the moment.

Billy wiped his eyes again and struggled to focus. “I’m sorry, I don’t remember much else.”

Dawn leaned over and rested her head against Billy’s arm. She was about to say something when the cafeteria doors opened once again and Burt rushed in.

The coroner approached the table still dressed in scrubs with his mask pulled below his chin. Everyone stared back, holding their breath, waiting to hear the horrible news. “You need to come with me,” he said to Wendy and Troy. “Janis is awake, and she asked for you.”

CHAPTER 93

Don and Stephanie stood outside the back entrance of the sheriff's department amidst a splattering of black stains that blanketed the lot. The security door lay buckled, torn from its hinges and shattered frame. A thick trail of the tar-like substance, left from a thousand different prints, led into the building as far as either could see.

"Hello," Don called into the seemingly quiet building. "Is anyone there?"

Stephanie followed close behind Don as he maneuvered a path around the broken door and entered the basement hallway. The couple navigated the aftermath of what could only be described as a war zone. Broken ceiling tile and light fixtures littered the floor, drywall and plaster had been ripped free from the walls, and furniture from the basement offices lay pulverized in splinters. The hallway intersected at a T; they turned right and followed until they came to a dead end. A heavy door with the word Armory written on it had been left open.

The door was intact for the most part; it had taken a beating with a rippling of dents on its surface but didn't appear to have been compromised in any way. An optimistic swell stirred within Don but was quashed when he entered the armory. He scanned the empty shelves and gunracks, then noticed the blood-soaked mattress in the far corner. Stephanie saw it only a second later and cried out. She rushed toward the cot and stood over it, staring down as time froze.

They both sensed it, heavy in the air; the children had been there, and not that long ago.

"No," Stephanie sobbed. The stain covering the pillow and mattress was bright red but had already started to turn brown where it had dried along the edges. It spread out in a circular pattern approximately the size of a dinner plate and had obviously come from a traumatic wound. She turned to Don with ribbons of tears streaming down her cheeks. "My baby!" she cried.

"Hey," he said, taking her in his arms. "That could be anyone's blood. We don't even know if they were here." But Don sensed otherwise and could tell Stephanie did as well. He also knew there was only one place left for them to look: the medical center. He took her by the hand and started to head for the door but stopped when he felt the hard object catch in the tread off his boot. Don bent down and pulled it free. He stood up holding the shard of magnet that had been left on the floor.

The ambush that took place in the medical center's basement hadn't even lasted an hour and had ended in a bloodbath with the entire group being devoured in either the literal sense or in a far more perverse fashion. Those who hadn't been fed on were invasively consumed and then added to the brood. The men who assembled to defend the basement's only entrance had overlooked the breach in the elevator shaft and were taken by surprise. Somehow, they had managed to fell many of the enemy's forces. Bodies of the creatures now littered the basement floor, lying next to the remains of the firemen, nurses, and patients. However, not everything in the basement was dead.

A piece of something had been left behind ... forgotten. The beast had been injured but still held a glimmer of the master's essence. It lifted itself on broken leathery wings and dragged itself across the floor. Running on instinct, it inched forward toward the open elevator shaft and listened. The once great creature, born for flight, projected like a radar beacon and attempted to contact the hive.

Three sets of eyes woke from their sleep and focused on the wounded creature. They scanned the basement and listened to the echoes resonating in the air. It was nearby, a presence they had been searching for. Their force spread out, dividing into three separate units, and dispersed throughout the building like a vapor. It covered the basement, where all was quiet, then traveled up the shaft to the roof, only to find more death and rot. It carried up the stairwell, entered the lobby, and detected what it was looking for. It rushed further into the building, travelled down a hallway, and found the room where the simple ones were gathered. It was here ... the boy was here.

It watched the child and listened to the thoughts of the others until it located something it could use. It zeroed in on the group's weakness and allowed its essence to return to the creature in the basement. Still strong enough to trigger the snare. Soon, it would be even stronger, with fresh vessels to carry its presence forward.

Doris and Michelle Marks stepped from behind the curtain and met Troy, Wendy, and Lois as they approached with Burt leading the way. The head nurse lowered her mask and leaned down to face the children.

"I don't know if she will be awake for long, but she wants to talk to you both." Doris turned to Lois and nodded. No one had expected Janis to survive, let alone regain consciousness. She opened the curtain and allowed the children and Lois to enter the small area while she and Michelle waited behind.

Troy approached the side of the bed and stared down at his friend. She looked small to him, thinner and weaker than he remembered, like she had wasted away overnight. A fresh bandage had been wrapped around her head, covering the entire left side of her face, including her eye. Purple bruises crawled out from under the thick gauze and stretched across her face from her nose to her cheek. When Troy touched the side of the bed, Janis's right eye fluttered, then opened, bloodshot and foggy; he wondered if she could even see through it at all. Then a faint smile creased her lips and she attempted to turn toward him, but the mountain of ice packs surrounding her head prevented her from moving.

"Y-you scared us," was all he could say, the bulge in his throat oppressively choking off the words.

Wendy slid beside him and took Janis's hand. She had already been crying, but now the flow was ceaseless.

"Why are you crying?" Janis said in a voice as frail as a teardrop. "Did I miss Halloween?"

Wendy and Troy managed to laugh.

"No, it's still a few days away," Troy said. "But I never made my costume."

Janis looked up at Wendy. "Boys," she hissed, then closed her eye and lay still.

Troy and Wendy were sure she had fallen asleep again and didn't know if they should stay, until Janis stirred and opened her eye as much as the swollen lid would allow. She looked up at them and tried to raise her head. "Watch out," she said, her voice trailing off and the words impossible to understand. "Troy." She struggled to shrug off the crashing waves of exhaustion.

There was a long pause as Janis winced; a tortured look crossed her face as if she were attempting to hush an army of jackhammers pounding inside her head. Michelle pulled back the curtain and approached the bed. "I'm sorry, but your friend needs her rest. You should probably go now."

"No!" Janis shouted and latched on to Wendy's hand. "Watch out for the bad woman! You need to watch out for the—"

"She doesn't know what she's saying," Michelle said. "She's delirious."

"Troy." Janis lowered her stare and spoke in a voice that sounded nothing like her own. "Y-you have to get all of them ... t-the Ojanox. You have to get it all ... every scrap."

Janis closed her eye and fell back against the pillow as her friends stood beside the bed, looking at her and then at one another. Troy was certain that Janis knew exactly what she was saying and hadn't been delirious. The mention of the creature's name was all the proof they needed. Still, he had no idea what she had meant about the woman. "What bad woman?" he asked, but Janis had fallen asleep.

Michelle and Doris moved to usher the children out of the emergency area and adjust the ice packs surrounding the girl's head. Troy stayed a moment longer and placed his hand on top of Wendy's and Janis's. "Don't worry," he told her. "We'll get all of them. We'll get every last scrap."

CHAPTER 94

The late morning sun reflected off King Lake like a million diamonds caught in a ripple of wind. From where Günter stood on the north shore, it looked like a perfect autumn day, but after surviving the past twenty-four hours, he knew it was anything but perfect. The town where he had chosen to raise his children had been erased in a heartbeat.

He opened the garage doors of the rec center and instructed his crew to back their vehicles up to the boats where they'd been stored for the winter. The three sloops had been winterized and stowed away less than a month ago, and there was little work to do to get them ready.

The first boat was backed into the water; Andrea, Richard, and Tyler busied themselves by gathering every life preserver and flotation device available. Most of them were child size, which was fortunate, since the majority of the passengers were under twelve. There were no older children among the small group of survivors, as most of the teenagers hadn't shown up to the shelters and probably hadn't taken the threat seriously. It was a shocking contrast to see an entire demographic of the population absent.

Billy Tobin and Cyndi, the candy striper, were the only surviving members of their age group.

Anthony Leone released the catch on the back of the trailer, and the second boat slid gently into the water. Hazel and the Bentley girls pulled it to the dock, then tied the bow and stern lines to the cleats. Even Marylin pitched in and did her part, who was the youngest and had been around boats since the day she was born. The three girls shouted and ran around the dock like it was just another day at the lake.

Günter watched his wife and daughters, their laughter causing his heart to ache. He doubted that any of the adults in town would ever laugh like that again. No one would ever get over what had happened. With two boats already in the water and the third one close behind, Günter was anxious to get underway. As much as he had loved this town and the roots that he and his family had planted, he knew that once he reached the other side of King Lake, he would never return to Garrett Grove.

Lois stared at the empty chairs where she and Troy had sat waiting to hear news of Rob's condition. It all started just six days ago, not even a full week to the day. They had rushed Rob to this very emergency room; at the time, it appeared to be a severe case of the flu. They had sat in the waiting area trying to make sense of it all. But there wasn't any sense to be found, not in a world where an entire town could be wiped off the map in less than a week.

No one noticed the man and woman when they entered through the emergency room doors and stopped. They waited for a moment with neither one saying a word, staring at the group that had assembled near the parted curtain. Don Fischer and Stephanie Thompson looked across the empty room to see Lois, Troy, and the young dark-haired girl gathered in an embrace. Scanning the area, both of their eyes fell onto the child laying on the bed. Stephanie's gasp sliced through the air like a surgical blade.

"God. No!" Stephanie screamed and rushed past Don to where the group was gathered. She pushed her way through Doris and Michelle and latched on to her daughter's bed. "Janis!" Her cries penetrated the emergency room in a despondent echo, affecting the others as if it were happening to them, as if Janis were not just Stephanie's daughter but all of theirs. Doris followed the woman behind the curtain and attempted to explain what had happened. How Janis had been involved in a car accident and how they had done everything they could for her. She explained how Janis had regained consciousness and spoken to her friends, which was a great sign. And although it was too soon to tell, judging from her speech and eye movements, Doris told Stephanie she was cautiously optimistic and that Janis was a very strong little girl.

Stephanie clung to her daughter's hand and lay her head next to her on the bed. Her breath burned in her lungs, and her eyes blurred from the onslaught of salty tears. Now more than ever, she was convinced that her own actions had brought this upon her daughter. *I did this to you, baby.* "Janis, I'm so sorry, baby. This is all my fault."

Troy looked up as Dr. Thompson ran past him, then saw his father standing near the entrance. For a moment, time stood still, then Don rushed toward his wife and son with his arms spread open. He scooped Lois, Troy, and Wendy into his arms and pulled them into a great bear hug. He kissed Lois on the forehead and squeezed them even tighter. "Oh, God. I thought I lost you."

"I knew you were all right." Troy looked up into his father's tear-soaked eyes. "I just knew it."

"I love you, kiddo," he said, reaching into his pocket and pulling out the small black magnet. He held it for them to see. "I followed your trail, from our house to the sheriff's department, and then here."

Lois searched to find the words. She held on to her family with the massive lump in her throat threatening to stop her breath. Her bottom lip trembled, and her arms shook uncontrollably; she tried to catch her breath but was unable. The world was moving at light speed, and the emotions washing over her were impossible and confusing. Loss, despair, hopelessness, and regret were compounded and juxtaposed by gratitude and an overwhelming sense of joy. Her son and husband were safe, which was a godsend, but it didn't feel real or even fair, not when so many others were gone. Alice, Will, Eric ... the entire town. Lois listened to the woman behind the curtain. Stephanie's sobs stabbed at her, and her own heart cried in harmony.

She offered Don an all-knowing look. Despite the rift that had grown between them, they were acutely in tune with one another. He nodded back to her, then looked off toward the part in the curtain. "If you kids would excuse us for a second, I think Janis's mother could use our support." He tossed Troy's hair and then turned to the dark-haired girl. "It's nice to meet you, Wendy. I'm Don."

Wendy and Troy took each other's hands as Don and Lois disappeared behind the curtain. It was hard to hear what was going on exactly, but they could see the shadows of the adults when they came together in an embrace.

The other members of the group watched the scene from the lobby. Jessica Marceau, Billy, Cyndi, and Carl gathered with Dawn and Baxter, watching the emotional events unfold. Jessica had begun to cry like everyone else, turned to Billy and excused herself, then made her way down the hall in search of a ladies' room. She rounded several corners and continued to walk until she found herself in an unfamiliar corridor. *This isn't the way I came.* She turned back. *And it sure isn't the way to the ladies' room.* She passed a set of double elevator doors labeled Freight and continued walking. Finally, she found it. She opened the door and entered the pitch-black darkness; Jessica froze with the door closing behind her.

Her heart raced, the overwhelming murk filling her with a sense of disorientation. She reached toward the wall beside the door and fumbled for the light switch, praying the emergency electricity was working in this part of the building. Her hand found what she was looking for and flipped the switch; one of the overhead fixtures sizzled to life, illuminating the lavatory in a dim glow.

Jessica stepped across the tile floor and entered the nearest stall. Closing the door behind her, she sat down, buried her face in her hands, and wept. She tore off a wad of tissue and used it to blot the tears from her skin. She struggled to control her breathing, knowing if she didn't get a hold of herself, she would hyperventilate. *Deep breaths in ... deep breaths out.* She focused and fought to make any sense of what was happening; there was little to be found.

The bathroom door creaked, causing Jessica to jump. She drew her hand over her lips to stifle the sound of her sobs. Holding her breath, she waited for whoever it was to enter the room. The door slammed with a loud thud, and a second later, the room went dark. Blackness wrapped around Jessica like a shroud. She sat frozen with her heart slamming against the inside of her ribcage; she could sense the person standing there in the dark. She nearly screamed when the first footstep fell against the floor. It sounded like a wet mop being thrown against the tile, sloppy and out of place. It was followed by a second, and then she smelled it, sour, foul, and oppressive. The stench of rotting fish permeated the room; the underlying tang of dank fungus smelled as if it were full of intent.

Tears fell from her cheeks onto the floor, but Jessica remained motionless, praying her presence hadn't been detected. Another wet slopping of waterlogged flesh slapped against the tile and approached the stall where she sat. The offensive stench grew stronger, turning her stomach; she knew she was about to lose what little breakfast she had eaten. It stopped at the door in front of her, followed by the sound of a steady dripping. Water rained onto the floor less than a foot away, peppered by the occasional splats of something falling that was a bit more solid. Jessica tried not to visualize the presence, but thoughts of a beast standing before her dropping pieces of its rotting flesh were impossible to sequester.

A wet thud slapped against the door, causing Jessica to jump where she sat. A second thud splattered against the steel and almost sent the door flying inward. A low hiss crept through the air and morphed into a gargle. A million scenarios raced through the mayor's mind—fighting, escape, surrender—but none that she could act on. She sat frozen as the beast pressed its rotted face against the stall door.

"Jessica—" it hissed, just before the door crashed inward.

Amy Sterling waited in the lot at Mountainside Park, leaning against the hood of her Corolla, smoking one Virginia Slim after the next. She hoped at least some members of the parish might return. But the distant sound of gunfire echoing off the top of the mountain hadn't lasted long, nothing like the epic battle the congregation had anticipated. Still, she held out hope that Julie had been spared and would soon return.

After two hours of silence with no sign of anyone, Amy knew the entire group had been slaughtered. There was no need to stick around any longer; no one was coming. She flicked her cigarette butt into a dry patch of brush and prayed it might catch fire and torch the entire mountain. Then she got in her car and drove down Mountain Ave for what she knew would be the last time. She never looked in the rearview at the torn down fence that once blocked the old road as it faded from view.

The drive back into town was surreal; Garrett Grove had been devastated in the short time Amy had been away. The roads were deserted, with no sign of life in any of the developments she searched. She drove by her place but was too afraid to go inside after discovering several bodies in the road outside the house. A trail of remains spread out from her driveway to the front lawn on the opposite side of the road. Amy couldn't bear to imagine what she might find inside and just kept driving. She had given up hope of locating any survivors but decided to head to the sheriff's department anyway.

When she reached the Turnpike, a reflection in the distance caught her attention; a glint of light flashed off the windshield of a Ford pickup pulling out of the municipal building's parking lot. Amy followed the vehicle from a safe distance, not wanting to alert the driver to her presence, at least not yet. She crept along while the pickup gained speed and turned onto Mandeville. It passed the high school, then veered into the medical center's parking lot, taking the turn a bit too fast and nearly colliding with a parked Jeep. Amy eased her car to the side of the road and watched the man and woman exit the truck and rush into the emergency room entrance.

Amy lit another cigarette and prepared to follow them. After her experience with Father Kieran and the church of the holy kamikazes, she was reluctant to rush in for fear of finding another group of unhinged lunatics. But the idea of remaining alone in the ghost town of Garrett Grove was even less appealing. About a half hour and several cigarettes later, she stood at the emergency room door, working up her courage to go inside. Amy pitched her last butt onto the walkway and entered the building.

Most who had gathered in the cafeteria to listen to the sheriff's evacuation plans made use of the amenities the center had to offer. The senior demographic found a few quiet rooms and helped themselves to the empty beds. Jill Boriello and Brandon Canfield used one of those beds for an entirely different reason; their lovemaking served as an act of celebration for having survived the night. Although Jill had never been the type to sleep with a man she just met, today was no ordinary day, and she knew she might never get the chance to do it again.

Carl had excused himself and headed off to freshen up as well. Now sitting at a table in the back of the room, Burt, Ted, and Bob drank coffee in silence. The soothing warmth of the brandy Burt provided helped take the edge off the moment as each man prepared himself for the night they were about to face.

"I'm guessing the high school is still the safest place to holed up." Bob took a long sip from his mug.

"The boats aren't coming back, are they?" Burt asked, but already knew the answer. It would be suicide for them to even try. Ted and Bob didn't answer, but each offered the old man a look that spoke volumes. "Yeah, I figured as much. Well, I've got some more brandy back at the office; we can stop there on our way to the high school."

"I'll drink to that." Ted raised his mug. "I took a mental note of everyone in the room. We'll get most of them out with only one trip ... well, since the seniors decided to sit it out."

"I'm not very comfortable allowing them to make that decision," Burt said.

"You can't force them if they don't want to go." Bob leaned back and squinted. "What they did ensures that all the women and children will survive. You got to respect that, even if you don't agree with it."

Burt nodded, knowing the chief was right. And now that the liquor was nearly gone, a silence fell over them, with each man thinking the same thing. What chance did they have of lasting another night? There weren't enough men left to defend the shelter, not with less than ten guns against a few thousand of those things. Burt could sense Bob's apprehension at the idea of heading back into the shelter, and for good reason. The place would be ripe by now. And it was obvious that Ted wasn't about to step foot into the center's basement. The young officer had tensed up at the very mention of it. As far as Burt was concerned, he figured he would go wherever Carl and Doris did, wherever that might be. He was never the greatest soldier and certainly not the brightest by a long shot, but when it came to loyalty, Burt knew he was as faithful as a Golden Retriever.

Carl entered the cafeteria looking a good deal better than he had before he left. His hair was wet, and he now wore a fresh set of cloths he liberated from the janitorial closet—green work pants and a matching shirt with a name tag that read Theo. The men did a double take, finding it strange to see him in anything other than his uniform.

Carl approached the table, his keen power of perception kicking in when he spotted the three empty mugs. "Guess I missed the party," he said and winked.

Burt reached into his jacket and pulled out the flask. "Saved ya a pop." He offered it to his friend, giving the contents a shake. Carl's eyes widened, and he accepted the gesture, taking a seat at the table and finishing off what was left.

"Gentlemen." He checked his watch; it was just after eleven. "We should be hearing from Mr. Bentley any minute now. I want everyone we can fit on those boats." He turned to Burt. "I suppose I'd be wasting my breath if I told you I wanted you on one of them."

"You know you would," Burt said. "Besides, who would watch your back if I left?"

Car laughed. "Well, just try not to shoot me while you're busy watching my back."

"I'm not making any promises."

"If you don't want Burt to shoot you," Ted added, "just stand in front of him."

Carl and Burt turned their heads with a jerk and looked at the young deputy in disbelief; it had been more than a little out of character for Ted to say such a thing. The young deputy shifted in his seat, a flush of red spreading across his cheeks and forehead. "I-I didn't mean anything by that, M-Mr. Lively."

The sheriff and coroner exploded with a gale of genuine laughter that was contagious. Bob joined in, and even Ted relaxed, shedding a bit of his shell.

"He's got you pegged, Burt." Carl slapped Ted on the back with tears forming in the corners of his eyes.

Burt wrinkled his nose and lifted his upper lip. "He's got you pegged, Burt," he mocked. "Don't you have a toilet to scrub, Theo." He pointed to the name tag on the janitor's uniform. Which led to a fresh round of laughter that left them all catching their breath. It lasted for a few minutes until it ebbed and then passed. The men sat at the table waiting for whatever might happen next, certain the mood was about to shift.

"I got to be honest with you." Carl lowered his voice. "We're outnumbered a thousand to one, and I don't think the doors at the high school will hold them back for long. This probably doesn't end well."

A hush fell across the table, and no one spoke for what felt like far too long. None of them noticed the boy and the young woman who had been standing there long enough to hear everything Carl had said.

"Then why don't you do something about it instead of just hiding like it's already over?" Billy Tobin stood with one of the waitresses from the diner.

The men stared back at their new arrivals. Carl's face went slack like he'd been slapped as Billy continued.

"You have the chance to act, but all you want to do is go hide again. Well, hiding doesn't work with these things. It's time to get off our asses and go after them already."

"Now look here, kid," Burt raised his voice. "We're all upset, but you can't come in here and talk to the sheriff like that."

Carl raised his hand and stopped his friend. "It's all right, Burt. He's got every right." Carl turned to Billy Tobin. "I get it. But there are thousands of those things out there, and once the sun sets, they have the upper hand. They're stronger, and faster, and strategic. I have no idea how to fight something like that."

"That's because you're thinking conventionally."

Carl straightened in his chair and stared back, slack-jawed. "What did you say?" It was as if Billy Tobin had extracted the very thought from his head.

"You can't fight these things on even ground. You can't fight them face-to-face, and you can't run and hide ... You'll lose every time."

Ted and Bob exchanged a quick look, then turned back to hear the rest of what the kid had to say.

"I take it you have a suggestion?" Carl pinched the bridge of his nose and winced.

"Yeah! Hit 'em while they're sleeping. We go in and wipe them out before the sun sets, before they have the upper hand."

"And how do you propose we do that? There's a whole lot of ground to cover on the top of that mountain, and we don't even know where to start."

Billy turned to Amy Sterling. "We know exactly where they are, Sheriff. They're hiding in the sanatorium."

It had been right in Carl's face the entire time, and deep down, he thought he had probably known it all along. *Son of a bitch ... of course!* Where else would they be hiding? The place was a fortified complex and the only structure big enough to house that many bodies. He had overlooked the obvious and never considered taking the fight to the enemy. The kid was right; Carl knew he'd been thinking conventionally and had lost every battle because of it.

"You all know Amy." Billy nodded to the girl he had walked in with. "I think you'll be interested in what she has to say."

Amy cleared her throat and began to share her story with the sheriff and the rest of the men. She told them how she showed up at the church with nowhere left to turn and been recruited by Father Kieran into going to war against the creatures. She described everything the best she could, how the priest and his followers had turn fanatical. "It felt like I had joined a cult." Amy went on to say how she faked twisting her ankle to save herself, and that Father Kieran had left her behind on the side of the road. "I walked to my car and waited for them, hoping at least someone had made it. Then I heard the gunshots." She wiped her cheeks. "It didn't last long at all, and if they did what they had gone up there to do, there would have been a lot more shooting. So, I left, and I came here."

Carl listened with a mixture of shock and disbelief plastered across his face. He couldn't believe the priest had attempted such a thing with an army that possessed little to no fighting experience. Father Kieran had gone off the deep end, but he had attempted to do what none of them had even thought to try. It was a goddamn foolish thing to do but one of the bravest ventures Carl had ever heard of. He turned to Billy and squinted. "Let me get this straight. You want to go running up there just like Father Kieran and get us all killed?" Carl lowered his head and rubbed at his temples. *Fantastic, now this damn headache is back!* Billy Tobin had been giving him one for years.

"Not at all," Billy explained. "They went barging into the place with guns blazing… That's why it got them. You said it yourself; it's stronger, it's faster, and it's smarter. We can't go rushing in like the Magnificent Seven; we have to strike unconventionally."

"It knew we were coming," Amy said.

"Why do you think that?" Carl focused on the girl.

"Last night, they attacked the church and got Allison. They crashed through one of the windows and carried her away. After they took her, they backed off, like they had found what they came for."

"You think they wanted Allison?"

"I think it wanted something inside her ... information. Allison knew what Father Kieran intended to do. And if it can get inside your head, then maybe it read Allison's mind and decided it would be smarter to just wait for us at the sanatorium, rather than sacrificing a bunch of its soldiers trying to get into the church. We were doing a damn good job defending the place."

Jesus Christ, if that don't make a lot of fucking sense! Carl stared at Amy and Billy as the pieces clicked into place. *That's why Dr. Malcolm was sent to take out the MRI machine, and how Rainey knew to grab the heavy artillery before showing up at the high school. The goddamn thing is using our own intel against us.* "Okay. But what makes you think we'll do any better if we step inside that place?"

"You're still not looking at this right, Sheriff," Billy said. "We need to use guerilla warfare. We can't rush in there; they'll drop us before we draw our weapons. We got to torch the place from the outside ... You know, burn it to the ground."

"I have a better idea!" Don Fischer stood in the doorway with Dawn and Baxter at his side. Lois and the rest of the kids followed in a moment later. Don approached the table where the sheriff and the other men sat. "I have enough dynamite to level that place ten times over. That's how we take them out. We go up there and plant enough TNT to bring down half the mountain."

Carl opened his mouth to speak but was interrupted by a blare of static.

"Sheriff," Günter's voice crackled over the radios. "Ve are ready at the lake." Carl looked at Don and then at Billy. He smiled and nodded his head. As much as he hated to admit it, he knew the kid was right. It was an unconventional approach, and a damn good one. Not to mention, they were out of options. Carl's smile grew even wider. *This could actually work.*

CHAPTER 95

Günter and his team had successfully launched all three of the vessels, inspected the safety equipment and the riggings, and deemed the boats seaworthy before placing the call to the sheriff; they were ready to sail. The wind was in their favor, which would shave a little off the estimated time of their journey, but Günter knew that could change in a flash on the open water and didn't put much stock in it. He watched the first car pull into the entrance, kicking up gravel and dust as it came to a stop in front of the rec center. Miss Davis and Jill Boriello sat in the front seat, with Kelly Rainey and two other children from the elementary school riding in the back.

"Ahh Sehr Gut," Günter said, making the sign of the cross on his forehead. He waited for the rest of the passengers to arrive, remaining as patient as he could. But the sooner they set sail, the better; Günter was more than a little anxious to put Garrett Grove several nautical miles behind him.

“She’s stable at the moment,” Doris explained, with Stephanie hanging on every word. “But your daughter shouldn’t be moved. Even under the circumstances, I strongly recommend she remains here. The trip could kill her.” Michelle and Burt nodded in agreement; Cyndi stood by and offered her own support. “Mr. Lively and I will remain here. We’ll take good care of Janis.”

“You can join us,” Michelle said. She and Cyndi would be acting as the medical staff for those travelling in the boats. Once again, they were splitting the teams in half, hopefully with better results than they had had the first time.

Stephanie pressed her lips together and shook her head. “Thank you, but I’m not leaving. My place is here with my daughter, and I have a feeling there are others who are going to need my help.”

No one expected her to say anything otherwise. A stillness fell over the group where they stood just a few feet from Janis’s bedside; there wasn’t much left to say.

“Well, we should be on our way.” Michelle lifted the large medical bag at her feet and turned to the candy striper.

Cyndi was unable to keep her emotions in check quite like Michelle; she had never learned how to flip that switch. She grabbed Doris and hugged the old nurse with a fierce grip, then with a quiver in her lip and tears in her eyes, she hugged the others. “Please be careful,” she said before turning and following the paramedic out the side entrance.

“Thank you, Nurse TenHove, Burt,” Stephanie said, holding herself together as best she could. “You saved Janis’s life. I could never repay you for that." She took in an icy breath and placed her hand on her daughter's bed. "Unfortunately, I have to ask one more thing from both of you."

"You don't have to ask," Burt said and nodded his head in agreement.

"We'll take good care of her," Doris said.

Stephanie excused herself and made a beeline toward the cafeteria.

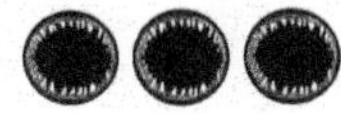

"You know I have to do this," Don explained to his family and the extended members. Wendy and Dawn occupied the seats next to Lois and Troy, with Baxter sleeping on the floor at their feet. "I'm the only one qualified to handle explosives." He tried to reassure them before they left for the boats.

"You just came back to us," Lois said with tears in her eyes. "I don't like anything about this plan."

"That's why I need to make sure these cowboys don't kill themselves. I know I'm not the hero type, but if there's one thing I'm good at, it's blowing stuff up."

"Carl knows explosives," she said, wiping her cheek. "He was a demolitions expert in the war."

Don winced and bit his lip. "I don't think you ever told me that."

"Well." Lois wrung her hands and scanned the room. "I know he doesn't like to talk about it, and it really wasn't my place to say."

"Doesn't matter." Don waved his hand and continued. "They didn't use dynamite in Vietnam, anyway. It was either C-4 or ANFO, which is the same principle, but trust me, it's not the same at all. Not to mention, that was over ten years ago. Even if he knows what he's doing, he's more than a little out of practice. I do this every week. You know I'm the most qualified."

"Dad's right, Mom." Troy lifted his head and looked up at Don. "Nobody's better at it than Dad."

Lois forced a smile and let out a long slow breath.

"I love you, guys," Don said. "Don't worry, we're going to get this thing."

"You got to get all of them." Troy's eyes widened as he spoke. "You can't miss even one; you have to get them all."

"Every scrap," Wendy added, wrapping her arm around Dawn and pulling the girl close.

"You don't have to worry about that. By the time the smoke clears, half the mountain will be gone, and every last one of those things will be dust." He leaned back in his chair and offered the group a wide smile.

Lois lowered her voice and leaned in. "And how do you plan on doing that without those things figuring out what's going on?"

He opened his mouth and then shut it just as quickly as Carl, Ted, and Billy approached the table.

"Sorry to interrupt. It's time for the rest of you to head out; the boats will be leaving shortly." Carl addressed Lois and the children, then leaned in and spoke to Don. "I'm anxious to hash out the particulars of the plan with you and the other men when you're ready. There's six of us. I'm not a big fan of that number, to be honest; I'd feel a whole lot better with a lucky seven."

Don shrugged his shoulders and nodded in reply.

"We're almost ready," Lois said, offering the children her bravest smile, then looked around the cafeteria for the missing member of their group. "Has anyone seen the mayor?"

"I just passed her in the hall," Stephanie said; no one had heard her enter the cafeteria. She approached the table and stared the sheriff in the eye. "I'm coming with you." Her words fell like mortar fire.

"I don't think—"

"Think what, Sheriff? It's a good idea? What isn't a good idea is going up there without a clue of what you're up against. Just how do you plan to get close enough without those things knowing you're there?" She stood like a tree with her hands on her hips, staring at Carl as if he were a little boy.

Carl turned to Billy and then to Don. "Well, we haven't fleshed out all the details yet. I'm guessing you have a suggestion, Dr. Thompson?"

"As a matter of fact, I do."

"She knows a whole lot more about these things than any of us, Sheriff," Don said. "I'd listen to her."

Carl pinched the bridge of his nose and scanned the members of his group. There was little time to argue. "Looks like you're our seventh man." He smiled and looked down at Don. "So, to speak." Then, checking his watch, he turned back to Lois. "You really need to get moving."

Jessica Marceau rushed into the cafeteria like a breeze. "Sorry I took so long." She rummaged through her purse. "You know, girl stuff."

Dawn stood up and grabbed Baxter by the leash. She walked him over to Ted and wrapped her arm around the deputy's leg. Ted bent down and hugged her back. "I'm gonna miss you, honey. Have fun on the boat."

Dawn allowed him to straighten the oversized deputy hat she still wore, then she took the end of Baxter's leash and placed it in his hand. "Janis is going to need someone to watch over her. Baxter can keep her company while I'm gone." The slightest tremble took hold of her bottom lip as she scratched the dog behind the ears, then kissed him on the head. "Be a good boy," she said, then allowed Ted to hug her one last time.

The deputy wiped his cheeks and stood up with the leash in hand. The three of them had been through a lifetime together in only a few short days, and the bond that had developed between them was as strong as iron.

"You really need to be leaving," Carl urged them, looking at Jessica. "Now."

"Gotcha," the mayor said, pulling a set of keys from her purse. "I'll drive."

Lois approached Billy and hugged him. "I don't like this at all, but I know there's no talking you out of it."

"Don't worry, Aunt Lois. I got nine lives."

"You're right about that," she said. "Just be careful and come back to me." Then she turned to Carl and cracked a smile. "You look like you haven't slept in a week."

"Maybe a bit longer than that," he said and raked his hands through a recently formed grey head of hair.

She threw her arm around her old high school sweetheart and kissed him on the cheek. "Take care of my family and watch your ass." She released him and turned to leave.

Troy reached into his jacket pocket and wrestled the item out. "Here you go, Dad. You might need this." He held out his wrist rocket and a handful of broken magnets. Don took them and wrapped his arms around his son.

"I love you, kiddo. I'm sorry I wasn't there to help build Scream in the Dark. I should have been there." Don knew he'd been a selfish prick and had messed up royally. He had missed every major development in his son's life and been an absent father at best. He didn't know if this was the second chance he had prayed for, but he wished that it could be.

"There's always next year," Troy said.

"Next year," he agreed, then stood up and faced his wife one last time. They shared a look that didn't require words. The weight of that one look was felt by both, as strong as an avalanche and as unstoppable as a raging river. Lois stood on her tiptoes and kissed him.

"Come back to us," she said.

The moment was broken when Wendy held up the items she'd been holding and offered them to Stephanie. The woman took the wrist rocket and handful of magnets and smiled back at the girl. "Thank you for taking care of Janis."

Carl cleared his throat loud enough for everyone to hear. He rested his hands on his utility belt and stood there dressed in his green janitor's uniform.

"Okay, we're leaving, Theo," Lois laughed, lifting the mood for a moment, then she and Jessica ushered the children along and left the cafeteria without looking back.

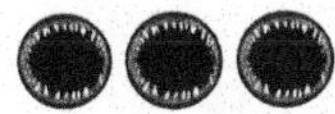

"If those things knew Father Kieran and his group were there, then what makes you think they won't know we're coming?" Ted asked once Lois and the others had left the room.

Stephanie looked at Don and then at Carl; she had an idea but thought she would keep it in the vault a bit longer.

"Actually ..." Billy smiled and leaned in. "We want them to know we're coming." Ted looked at him as if he were crazy. "We want them to know exactly where we are ... at least some of us."

The group hashed out the plan as best they could, but there was still a big piece of the picture that had been left out ... and for good reason. Stephanie knew it wasn't wise to share everything with everyone. Information was power when it came to this Entity, and the fewer who knew what she had in mind ... the better.

CHAPTER 96

Billy threw open the overhead door and entered the garage with Ted behind him. Afternoon sun flooded the two-car area reserved for tools, hunting gear, and the rest of the Tobin boys' hobbies. Will Tobin had lost the battle years ago and allowed his sons to take over the garage to store their collection of grown-up toys. Although lately the boys' interests had centered around girls, the items that Billy and Ted were looking for were something that the Tobin boys still made use of every weekend.

The two YZ 750 dirt bikes stood next to each other in the center of the garage. Billy and Eric had been riding since they were big enough for their feet to touch the ground. The trails that ran through the foothills and crossed the old extension had been the boys' stomping ground for years.

"Here." Billy pulled a large bin out from under a workbench and pried off the top. "You're gonna need these." He tossed several different sized pads and protective gear at Ted, who wasn't that much older than Billy and had spent just as much time on the trails as any boy in town. It was a mountain community, after all, and two things were guaranteed:

everyone owned a gun, and damn near every boy road a dirt bike. Ted began strapping on the knee and shin pads and was nearly dressed when Billy approached with a roll of duct tape.

"What do you plan on doing with that?" he asked.

"Trust me. This is gonna save your ass." Billy yanked at the tape and started to wrap it around the bottom of Ted's legs, over his calves and ankles, and even over the shin pads.

"Can you still move your foot?"

Ted twisted his ankle to check the range of motion and to make sure he would still be able to operate the brake and gears. "Yeah, it's good."

"Perfect." Billy tossed him a helmet, then wrapped the duct tape around his own legs. He didn't know exactly what to expect from the thing hiding in the old sanatorium, but he didn't believe it would behave any different than it had in the past. It was a hunter, and all hunters were creatures of habit. They found what worked, and they usually stuck to it; they never changed tactics once they found an effective method. At least that's what he was counting on; not only was he betting his own life on it but everyone else's as well.

"This is gonna work, right?" Ted asked.

"Oh yeah. This is gonna work." Billy tilted his head and shrugged. "Probably."

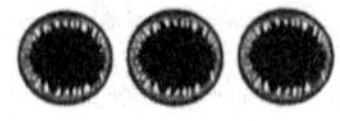

The pump truck droned like an oil rig as Bob Jones and Brandon Canfield made their slow approach up Mountain Ave. They rounded the curve just before the entrance of the park to find a line of vehicles on either side of the street and packed into the dirt lot as well; Father Kieran's forces had never returned to retrieve them. Two men on dirt bikes blocked the road where the old extension began. Bob turned off the truck and stepped out.

"Did you do that?" he asked, looking at the remains of the downed fence.

"Not us," Ted answered, pulling off his helmet. "Must have been the others. Saves us the trouble, I guess."

"Any word from the sheriff?" Brandon joined them.

"Not yet. It'll take some time for them to get in position. We could be waiting a while."

Bob looked at the duct tape covering the bottom half of the men's legs. "Don't suppose you got any more of that stuff?"

Billy unslung his backpack and pulled out a new roll. He tossed it to Bob, who went to work wrapping his own legs, then handed the roll to Brandon, who did the same.

"Better safe than sorry." Bob cast a tentative glance up the old road, then turned his head to the sky and shielded his eyes from the glare. It was a cloudless day, and that was about the best news they would get. He removed the walkie-talkie from his belt—it was still too soon to move forward, but he was as anxious as everyone else.

"How are you looking, Carl?" He watched the radio tremble in his hand; his nerves were working overtime. Scanning the faces of the other men, Bob offered an awkward smile of encouragement that may or may not have been effective. He prayed he was the only one who could tell just how nervous he really was.

Carl stood next to Stephanie at the passenger's side of Don's truck. They both jumped when Bob's voice crackled through the small speaker as they waited in silence for Don, who had disappeared behind the demolished remains of one of the trailers to retrieve the explosives. Carl had half anticipated the blast of a detonation when the radio transmitted.

"Yeah, Bob. We're at the quarry now and should be on our way in about fifteen minutes. We'll have to take it slow, though, at least an hour or so."

"Roger that," Bob replied. "We'll get started on our end. If anything happens or you get held up, let us know. Other than that, I guess we're going silent from here."

Stephanie had suggested that once they got started, they should cease all radio transmissions. She wasn't certain but implied the Entity might be sensitive to certain frequencies as it had been to the magnetic pulse of the MRI machine. If that was the case, there was a possibility it could track them through their own radio transmissions. Of course, it was just a theory, but Don agreed and said they would be wise to follow her advice.

"I got a feeling if anything goes wrong on our end, you won't need the radio to hear about it." Don had told them he was bringing enough TNT to blow up the sanatorium three times over. If something bad did happen, they would be hearing it as far as Warren.

"Just make sure nothing goes wrong, then," Bob said.

"10-4, over and out." Carl returned the radio to his hip. He had modified his gun belt to carry the .38 on his right and a .44 on the left, with as much ammunition as he could fit jammed into every available slot and pouch. He wore it over a set of jungle-design camo fatigues they had liberated from Harrison's Army and Navy. Stephanie wore an identical set cuffed at the ankles to prevent the legs from dragging on the ground, and Don had dressed the same. The group also covered their faces in camouflage grease paint to help blend into the mountain. No one knew if the extra precautions would make a difference, but they figured it couldn't hurt.

Carl scanned the quarry and the large section of the mountain that had been removed by DuCain industries. "Where is this cave located?"

Stephanie pointed to the left, where Gail had been killed. "Just over the rise of that slope." She could see the body of the scorpion creature that had attacked them.

"You've really been studying this thing your whole life?"

"Not my whole life," she said. "My father discovered it first on the Cahokia dig. He became convinced that something was responsible for the disappearance of the civilization. It's rarely spoken of, but the native tribes weren't the only ones who vanished. There was a major die-off during that period in every species—birds, mammals, reptiles. It had to be more than coincidental."

Carl rubbed his temples and swayed on his feet for a second. Stephanie reached out to steady him. "Are you okay?" she asked. "You look a little green."

The paint he had used to cover his face was in fact mostly green. "Very funny," he replied. "It's just a headache from not enough sleep."

"Yeah, I know what you mean." She continued: "The truth is, Sheriff, there are hundreds of lost civilizations that have simply vanished from the face of the earth. And there is more than a little evidence that suggests this Entity had everything to do with them."

"Just how old is this thing?"

She shrugged. "Ageless. I don't know, as old as time itself."

"I'm guessing we're not the first to try to take it out?" He removed a canteen from his belt and took a sip.

"We'll be the first to succeed." She offered a smile and a wink.

Carl wondered if she would be as optimistic in another hour or two. He watched Don Fischer emerge from behind the work trailer with a large pack on his back and one in each hand. He'd never cared much for the man who had taken his girl. Don appeared to be a self-absorbed prick who was all wrong for Lois. But watching the guy make his way across the quarry carrying enough dynamite to change the earth's rotation, Carl thought that maybe he had misjudged him.

"Okay, I got everything," Don said with sweat streaming from his brow.

"Are those packs fireproof?" Stephanie asked.

"Wouldn't matter if they were," Don answered. "Dynamite isn't. What you really need to worry about is if I fall or drop this stuff." He set the packs down and removed the gloves he wore, a thick pair with rubber hand grips.

"What are those for?"

"For handling the dynamite. You don't want to touch it with bare hands. It will really ruin your day, probably your entire week."

"We should get going," Carl suggested.

"Hold on a second." Stephanie removed her own backpack and set it on the ground. She opened the zipper and dug deep until she located what she was looking for. She stood up and held out the three ancient medallions. The gold links woven throughout the chain and emblem caught the sunlight and reflected it back like a crystal.

"When did you grab those?" Don asked.

"Before we left this morning. I thought they might come in handy." She placed one around her neck, the large ornate medallion covering a third of her chest. Then she held one with the chain open for Don to put his head through. He did, then tucked the large piece of jewelry under his shirt.

"What are those for?" Carl asked, staring at the artifact with a skeptical look on his face.

"Let's just say, I think this might be the best camouflage we could wear today."

He raised his eyebrows, thinking she was crazy, but decided to go along with it. He leaned over, and she slipped the gaudy medallion around his neck. It was large and bulky and heavy as hell, but the woman said to wear it and he would. Carl looked at the large bags Don carried and hesitated to interject.

"Do you need me to carry some of that stuff?"

"I've got it. You two should lead, and I'll follow behind from a distance. That way if something happens, I won't bury you in an avalanche or even worse."

Both Carl and Stephanie backed up a few steps. "Okay," Carl said. "It's been a few years, but I'm sure I remember the way. Once we crest the hill, we'll find the trails. Provided they're still there and not completely overgrown."

"Lead the way," Don said.

Carl walked toward the section of quarry that DuCain had been cutting into for the past decade. Stephanie fell in at his side, while Don waited until they were far enough ahead, then followed in their footsteps.

CHAPTER 97

Lois sat in the passenger's seat of the mayor's station wagon as they pulled out of the parking lot and turned right. She laid her purse next to her, then turned to Troy, Wendy, and Dawn in the back, who looked up and offered their best nervous smiles. They'd been through so much but were anxious to get out of town, maybe even a little excited to travel in the boats. Jessica, who sat behind the wheel, nodded to Lois, then reached into her own purse and started rooting around. Lois hoped she might be searching for a cigarette and had been craving one herself, although she didn't think the woman was a smoker.

The mayor continued to rifle through her purse, paying more attention to what she was looking for, and missed the turnoff for the lake. Lois watched as the woman passed the side street without so much as taking her foot off the gas. "You want to take Sunset to get to the lake," she said.

Jessica smiled in agreement but continued to rifle through her purse, making no effort to turn the car around or even slow down.

The mayor pressed her foot to the gas, causing the station wagon to lurch forward with a jolt. Lois turned to her and raised her voice. "I think you need to turn around. You're going the wrong way." Troy, Wendy, and Dawn looked up from the backseat; a cross between fear and confusion washed over their faces. Something was wrong.

Jessica pushed her foot harder to the floor, and the vehicle screamed in response. Trees, signs, and houses passed in a blur as the car sped to sixty miles an hour.

Lois's heart jumped into her throat. She reached out and braced herself against the dashboard. "What are you doing?" She couldn't imagine what had gotten into the mayor for the life of her. "Jessica, slow down. You need to go the other way!" Lois realized what was happening a moment too late.

The mayor's eyes clouded. A thin black film passed before them, blocking out the whites. Their natural appearance returned a second later, accompanied by an evil grin that spread across the woman's face like a sickness. Somehow ... it had gotten to her.

Lois tore at her purse to retrieve Carl's gun. She managed to pull open the flap, but that was all. The mayor drew back her hand and lifted her fist into the air. Lois saw the flash of something metallic in her grip but couldn't focus on it. The woman struck like a viper; Jessica slammed her fist into Lois's thigh and pressed.

Lois looked down at the hypodermic as Jessica depressed the plunger. The drug entered her body in a hot rush and took effect before she could react. First, she felt it in her face, flushing her cheeks and making her jaw go slack. Then her arms and legs grew heavy and went numb. Lois struggled to open her mouth, wanting to turn and warn the children, but was unable to move a muscle. She lost feeling in her torso as her head grew too heavy to hold up. She opened her mouth to scream, and a thin line of spit fell to her chin. Her head bobbed once, then twice, then fell against her chest, and Lois Fischer faded away.

Troy beat his fists against the back of the front seat. "What did you do to my mom?" he cried.

Jessica slammed the pedal to the floor, and the wagon took off like a rocket. She looked into the rearview mirror at the children, with the dark cloud filling the retinas of her eyes.

"Troooyyy ..." an inhuman voice hissed.

The children shrunk in the backseat, shaking and clinging to one another. Troy looked at the girls, searching for an answer but unable to think. "T-th-the bad woman," he managed with tears streaming down his cheeks. He stared at his mother's lifeless body in the front and sobbed. "Mom, get up. P-p-please, get up." But it was too late.

Wendy reached into her pocket for the wrist rocket, forgetting she had given it to Dr. Thompson. She started to cry as well and latched on to Troy and Dawn.

Jessica left the syringe sticking out of Lois's thigh. After being probed in the ladies' room at the medical center, the Entity had sent her on a mission. She had washed the ink-like fluid from her face before exiting, made her way past the cafeteria, and crept down the stairs leading to the basement. The shelter was littered with bodies, but it had been easy to locate what she was looking for. The stockpile of medicine had been left in the open. With the acquisition of Dr. Malcolm and the rest of the medical staff, the creature now possessed a full working knowledge of pharmaceuticals. Jessica found the vial easily and loaded several syringes with the fluid. She deposited them into the inner compartment of her purse, retreated the way she had come, and joined the others in the cafeteria.

Lois and the children had already been expecting her to drive, which made it even easier. Soon, it would reside in the new vessels; the three young hosts were strong enough to carry its essence to the next town. Finally ... it would have the one called Troy. It had tasted the boy in the graveyard and in the memories of Robert Boyle. Its hunger was acute and nearly blinding, but soon it would possess the object of its desire.

Three withered bodies lay shaking on the floor with the shared consciousness of the one pulsing through them. There was little left of their fragile shells. The protector stood watch over them, waiting for the new vessels to arrive. In a previous life, it had gone by the name of Butchie. But the massive creature that had been chosen for its brutality looked nothing like the man it had once been. After leaving the mind trap for the priest's army and retrieving a buried memory from deep within the Butchie creature, a suitable location revealed itself. A dark place of pain and suffering, one that the protector was familiar with. It was the perfect spot for the three to rest and would serve just as well for the transfer.

Günter checked his watch and paced along the shoreline. The boats were ready to sail, but they were still five passengers short. The sheriff had given him direct orders to depart no later than one o'clock, and it was already a quarter after. He had also been told to maintain radio silence and knew the sheriff and the others would be unreachable. Still, he knew he couldn't leave without the others and wrestled with the decision until he finally broke down and picked up the walkie-talkie. "Sheriff, dis ist Günter. Ve are still vaiting for ze last passengers to arrive. Ist anyone zerr?" The radio remained silent. "Please come in, Sheriff."

Günter exhaled and checked his watch again. He continued to make his final preparations as slowly as he could. The rest of the passengers were aboard, with the children tucked below decks. The equipment was stowed, and they were ready to leave. He walked to the third boat, where Tyler and Rich sat in the back at the transom.

"I'm afraid dis ist everyone."

"What about the rest? We still have room for five more," Rich said.

"Yes, yes, I realize zat." Günter nodded, then yelled to the next boat. "Andrea, please send Jerry over here." Then he called to his wife. "Hazel, please tell Michael to join us, sank you."

The two boys exited the other boats and boarded as instructed.

"Okay zen!" Günter shouted for everyone to hear. "Follow my lead und Gott bless you." Approaching the lead boat, he untied the bowline. He made his way to the back and released the stern line from the cleat. Then he pushed the boat away from the dock and jumped in. The sailboat floated out into the open water. Hazel lowered the keel as Günter raised the main sail until it was fully extended. The others followed, and the vessels were underway. Günter tacked the sheet into the wind, and the craft was propelled forward. Moments later, the boat was gliding across the water with Hazel steering them into the openness of King Lake.

Günter checked the dock, making sure the late arrivals had not shown up. But no car had entered the parking lot and there was no one on the dock. He watched the sandy beach in front of the rec center grow smaller and smaller until it became a speck on the horizon. Then Günter set his sights in the opposite direction and never looked back. With the wind at his back and the weight of guilt pressing even harder against him, he picked up the radio one last time.

It became a bit easier for the group to make headway after Carl navigated a passage out of the quarry. He led them up the carved-out face of Garrett Mountain, taking longer than he thought to find the trails. It had been years since he'd been up there, but once he gained his bearings, things started to look familiar. He stumbled across the first path, a bit more overgrown than he expected, and the memories of his youth came flooding back. It was still much like he remembered.

Don lagged a couple hundred feet behind, but after seeing the amount of dynamite the guy had liberated from the quarry, Carl couldn't help but wonder if even that was far enough. He continued to look back to check on the man, but Don Fischer followed at a steady pace and hadn't lost a stride. Stephanie surprised him as well, showing more energy and endurance than himself. The woman was clearly athletic and in great shape; Carl didn't know what sport she had played but knew there had been at least one. He could feel the lack of sleep and stress affecting his own performance, but he pushed himself to keep going. *Just a little bit longer,* he chanted, wiping the sweat from his brow.

The first trail led to a steep incline with close to a forty-five-degree upgrade. The hard-packed clay had been tamped down by the feet of the Lenape tribe centuries before any of his ancestors had set foot on the continent. Then one day, the tribe that lived on Lonesome Mountain disappeared without a trace. Stephanie followed behind Carl, stepping where he did, avoiding the loose gravel at the sides of the trail.

"This Entity," Carl said, looking over his shoulder at her. "How do you suppose it found its way here in the first place? I mean, after doing what it did at ... Cahokia, you say?"

"Good question," she said, matching his steps. "Best guess would be it hitched a ride on another life-form, maybe a deer that had become infected. It may have made a few stops along the way, or it could have come right here and then run into a member of the Lenape tribe. There's a painting of a holy man inside the cave; he could have been the first."

"Holy man?" Carl forced himself up the incline, his breath growing ragged in his chest.

"Yeah, and from there, it would have spread just like it did in Garrett Grove. But I'm willing to bet it never encountered a race quite like the Lenape."

"H-how do you mean?"

"Well, for one, they were in tune with nature on a spiritual level and believed in the healing powers of the mountain. Then there's the mineral deposits in the area. The Lenape had figured out a wa—" Stephanie almost ran into Carl, who had stopped short in front of her and blocked the path.

"Whoa," she said. "Are you okay?"

Carl bent over and clutched at his temple; his hands shook as he tried to catch his breath.

"Yeah, I just need a second." Carl squinted his eyes and tried to focus on the path before him, then everything went blurry. He swayed and caught hold of Stephanie. "It's my head; I've been getting these migraines for a couple days now."

Stephanie dug into her pack and removed a bottle of aspirin; she handed him three pills and her canteen.

"You're a lifesaver," he said, swallowing the tablets with a long gulp of water.

"Can never be too prepared."

"Hey, what's going on?" Don called from less than fifty feet away. He stopped and waited for them to continue moving. "Is everything all right?"

"Fine," Carl shouted. "Got a little dizzy for a second; better now. We're almost there, maybe another half an hour at most."

Don looked up the path to where Carl and Stephanie had stopped. He raised his arm and shrugged when she looked at him. *What's going on?* She shrugged herself. *I don't know.* He waited for them to continue and shifted the bags in his hands. It was bad enough that he and Buzzy had to relocate the explosives in the first place. But after the robbery, he had no choice. They had used one of the older storage areas and the temperature control wasn't half as good as it needed to be. The whole mess had been bouncing around for the past hour in the duffle bags, and it was turning into an unseasonably hot October day. Don had no idea if any of the sticks had already started to sweat and tried his best not to think about it. He watched as Carl righted himself and gave him a thumbs-up.

Come on. Let's get moving already. Don felt his heart thundering in his chest. The sooner he got this dynamite off his back wouldn't be nearly soon enough. A second later, Carl and Stephanie started moving again. He waited until they were a safe distance away, then followed in their footsteps. He felt the cold press of the lodestone medallion against his skin and wondered if it would have the effect Stephanie hoped it might. Not that he was willing to take it off and press his luck. *How much of this do you really know, and how much are you making up on the fly?* He couldn't help but second-guess Stephanie's call with the medallions. Figuring it best not to think too much about it, he told himself she knew what she was doing. *I'm only the guy carrying thirty pounds of dynamite; who am I to ask questions?*

Bob checked his watch and nodded to the other men; it was time to move. He took position behind the wheel, and Brandon slid into the passenger seat. Between them sat a pair of 12 gauge shotguns and a dozen boxes of shells. The men also wore sidearms and had brought almost a metric ton of ammo for both weapons. Bob gave Billy and Ted the go-ahead, then threw the truck in first and released the clutch.

Billy and Ted jumped down on the kick starts of the YZs almost simultaneously, and the bikes roared to life. Ted rechecked the shotgun hung against his back to make sure he still had easy access, then looked at Billy to do the same. Billy did, then hit the throttle and popped the clutch, causing the bike's front tire to jump twelve inches off the pavement. The YZ vomited a plume of gravel and dirt in its wake as Billy hotdogged it over the downed fence. Ted applied a bit less pressure, pulling a wheelie that only lifted about three inches. The deputy popped the bike into second, and Billy took off like a bullet ahead of him. Loose asphalt and silt, eroded from decades of weather and disrepair, was thrown into the air from their spinning tires. Ted pulled alongside Billy as the extension grew steeper and more treacherous. He motioned to the kid, shrugging his shoulders, not sure where to find what they were looking for. But the chief had gone over it with Billy, and the kid seemed to know what the man had been talking about.

The bikes ate up the incline with ease and had ascended almost half the distance to the crest when Billy veered to the left and slowed down. Ted spotted what he was headed for a second later. A small oval reflector sat on top of a fiberglass pole almost entirely obscured by the overgrowth of trees and brush. Billy led them straight to it and brought his bike to a halt;

Ted did the same. The sound of the pump truck shifting into lower gears screamed as the firemen made their way up the hill behind them.

Ted followed Billy, removing a small hatchet he had fastened to the handlebars of his bike. The men walked off the road into the tangled brush and found the ancient hydrant. It was thick with vines, buried under several feet of wild thorns. “Careful, those are the bastards that got me,” Billy said.

They made quick work of clearing the area, with Ted concentrating on the right side of the old plug and Billy focused on the left. They had just finished leveling the last of the vines when Bob pulled the pump truck parallel with the hydrant, blocking nearly the entire road.

Brandon jumped out of the passenger side and chocked the wheels, placing the huge wedges behind each one of the vehicle’s tires as Bob leapt from the vehicle and charged at the hydrant with the largest wrench Ted had ever seen. The big man attacked the fireplug and attempted to loosen the two-and-half-inch nuts on either side. He fitted the wrench to the cap on the right and leaned in with all his weight. It didn’t budge, not even a millimeter. Bob’s eye bulged as he realized how seized the rusted old plug had become. The department was scheduled to service hydrants on the extension once a year ... in a perfect world. But it had probably been closer to two or even three since this one had last been touched. It was also possible it had gone overlooked completely.

“Give me a fucking hand!” Bob shouted, standing up to catch his breath. Billy took the wrench in his hands and faced the chief. “Okay, one ... two ... three.” The two men leaned into the wrench; Billy lifted himself off the ground and came down against the strain.

The sound of metal grinding against metal echoed out of the old hydrant, and the cap began to move. The wrench slammed to the ground as the nut rotated a full quarter of a turn; Bob reaffixed the wrench, and the men went back to work. This time, the cap turned easier; the ancient metal squealed, then freed itself from its lock. Bob removed it the rest of the way without Billy's help, twisting the cap off one final turn before it fell to the ground.

He moved the wrench to the other side, and he and Billy went to work again. The left cap was equally as rusted, but now the men had an idea of how much torque was required to break the seal, and they managed to remove the second cap somewhat easier.

Sweat streamed down the chief's forehead and soaked the neckline of his shirt. He moved the wrench to the top of the hydrant and gave the others a look that suggested, *Here comes the hard part.* All three men grabbed the wrench and pulled it in a counterclockwise motion. The top cap turned almost instantly, much to everyone's surprise.

"Okay, we got it from here!" Bob shouted. "Time to do this." He went to work on the top of the old plug and counted out loud. "Seven ... eight."

Billy and Ted returned to their bikes, donned their helmets, and a moment later were spitting up twin fantails of gravel and dust; they sped away from the truck and continued up the old extension road.

"Ten ... eleven." Bob continued to loosen the plug on the top of the hydrant, and after the twelfth spin, he held his breath and turned the bolt for the thirteenth time. The sound of rushing water from deep within the underground pipe grew louder and louder until finally it erupted from the open caps on either side of the plug. It flooded the ground where Bob stood, dark and murky with massive flecks of rust and sediment throughout. It took a full minute for the water to filter out the debris and take on a clear transparency. After the last of the sediment dissipated, Bob turned off the water and grabbed the first piece of equipment that Brandon had set at his feet.

The Siamese connector resembled a large Y that attached to the hydrant at the two open caps on either side. Bob made quick work of it; he torqued down on the nuts, then took the pony connection and fastened it to the LDH that Brandon ran from the truck.

The pump truck carried approximately eight hundred and fifty gallons of water in its tank. Which would last about three minutes without a steady supply being fed to it. But that could be depleted much quicker if more hoses were connected and the man operating the deck gun got too overzealous.

Bob ran from the overgrowth and leaned into the cab of the truck. He exited a moment later with as much ammo he could carry and one of the shotguns. "Okay, get up there," he yelled to Brandon, who climbed onto the back of the truck. Bob handed him the weapon and supplies, then went back to the cab to retrieve his own gun. He set his weapon and several boxes of ammunition down on the guard of the truck and concentrated on the two lengths of hose that Brandon had set on the side of the road. Both were fifty feet in length with inch and a quarter smooth water nozzles that were powerful enough to remove the yellow line from the center of a highway. Today, they would be focusing the highly concentrated water pressure on something a bit softer than blacktop.

Billy crested the hill, throttled forward, and maneuvered a wide turn through the loop in front of the old sanatorium. Ted followed close behind, getting his first good look at the place in years. It was in far worse shape than the last time he had seen it, and he was overcome by an impending sense of dread. He examined the broken windows and crumbling steps of the facility, then focused on the entrance and the pair of shoes sticking out from the open front door. Squinting to get a better look, he noticed they weren't just a pair of random shoes but were attached to a set of legs. They jutted out the open door onto the porch while the remainder of the body lay concealed within the shadows of the building. Ted considered stopping for a moment to check if the owner of the shoes was still alive, then thought better of it. He knew the only thing that would accomplish was getting himself killed and jeopardizing the entire mission. He hit the throttle and sped through the turnaround to the back of the old parking lot.

Billy had told them what happened Sunday afternoon when he, Eric, and Mick attempted their half-assed assault on the sanatorium. And Ted kept his eyes peeled for movement as he navigated the dirt bike over the treacherous cracks and divots in the ancient asphalt. They made another pass through the turnaround in front of the building, and the deputy nearly dumped his bike when the first snake darted in front of his path. It was fast and startled him when it lifted its head to strike; he managed to maintain his balance and avoid what almost looked like a timber rattler. But there was something horribly wrong with the snake. It was disproportionate and had lost nearly all its coloring. The identifying rattler markings had faded as if the reptile had been bleached, with sections of its body so swollen it looked like it had swallowed several huge meals. But that didn't appear to slow it down; the snake quickly turned and struck out at Ted a second time.

He called ahead to Billy, who was already aware they had attracted the attention of the creatures. The kid swerved his bike in a zigzag pattern, navigating a path around a gathering of snakes that appeared to emerge from thin air. Within seconds, they were everywhere, to the left and the right of the men and blocking the way back to the road. Billy gunned the throttle, lifting his front tire off the ground. He rode the wheelie through the turnaround with his back tire chewing up snakes in its path. Ted followed the kid's lead as his front tire left the pavement in a sudden jerk. He was sure he would topple over, then eased on the gas and rode it out nearly as well as the kid. He felt the bodies squish beneath the weight of the bike as he made his way back to the road.

The serpents hadn't yet made it to the street when the two men took off down the mountain toward the truck, but it wouldn't be long. Ted fought the urge to look back for fear of losing control of the bike, and trusted the snakes would continue their pursuit. *I hope you're ready.* He prayed that Bob and Brandon could handle the holy hell that was headed their way.

The sound of dirt bikes cascaded over the mountain to where the small group ascended the final steps of their climb. Don brought up the rear with the added disadvantage of the heavy cargo he carried. Making sure each foot was well-placed before moving onto the next, he plodded along a safe distance behind Carl and Stephanie. He had taken care to pack things tight and secure, but it was still dynamite and unreliable under even the best conditions. You never wanted to think you were safe. The stuff sweat nitroglycerine and had a mind of its own, no matter how careful you thought you were. Don knew it wasn't the rookies who blew themselves up; it was the seasoned vets who grew careless over the years and lost respect for the stuff. He made his way to the top of the slope and came to the crest where Carl and Stephanie had stopped to watch from the cover of the tree line. Two men on motorcycles sped past the front of the building riding wheelies, then took off down the road.

From what Don could tell, the place looked quiet, with no sign of movement in any of the windows or at the front entrance. They were still a distance away and couldn't be sure, but he thought things looked good. They hadn't been attacked by anything like they had seen at the quarry, and so far, there was no sign of snakes. He looked at Carl, who checked his watch, then held up both hands with his fingers spread; in ten minutes, they would start. Don nodded as his nerves jangled with anticipation. He didn't like the idea of just sitting around with thirty pounds of dynamite, but at least Lois and Troy were out of harm's reach. By now, they would be close to halfway across King Lake.

CHAPTER 98

Jessica Marceau pulled the station wagon into the driveway where Marion Butchie Post once lived with his mother, Margaret. No longer in control of her own actions, the mayor operated under the same power that had directed Deputy Rainey to slaughter his own people. It had taken Jessica with very little effort, projecting its essence through the freight elevator shaft to the bathroom where it found the woman alone. It hadn't been there in the physical sense and merely slipped the woman a suggestion that festered like an infection inside her. The simple ones were that easy to control; however, some were more resistant than others. Rainey had been one of the easy ones, the first time, but the one named Ziegler had severed the tie. It was a bit more difficult to regain control the second time and had been necessary to ambush the deputy when he was alone to impose the full effect of its presence.

But with Jessica, it had been a seamless insertion, as if the woman had never been in control of herself to begin with, like she'd been waiting for direction. It slipped into her consciousness and manipulated the strings the way a child might do with a toy.

The woman bounded out of the car and tore open the back door where the children sat, causing them to scream and shrink away. The one called Troy reached over the smaller child and grasped at the door handle, but it was ripped out of his hand. The great beast stood before him. The creature that had started its life called Marion towered over the station wagon, nearly a foot and a half taller and far wider than it had previously been. The clothes it wore hung in tattered shreds from the gross expansion of its muscular and skeletal design. The creature's brow protruded over its eyes as if it were made of solid brick. It howled at the children, exposing a maw that contained at least two rows of jagged teeth.

It reached into the car, seized Troy and Dawn by the collars, and yanked them out of the back seat like bags of groceries. Jessica lunged at Wendy and removed the girl from the vehicle in a similar fashion, dangling the child in the air above the driveway like a ragdoll. Wendy kicked and struggled to break free from the woman's grip, but it was useless; the mayor was too strong.

"Let me go!" Troy screamed and was carried to the side of the house. He looked back in the direction of the car to see his mother's body slumped against the passenger side window. "What did you do to my mom?" The tears cascaded down his cheeks as he was carried away into the backyard.

"I'm gonna kill you!" Troy shouted as the gargantuan monster looked down at him and howled.

In the shed behind the Post house, the one called Ben turned its head in the direction of the mountain. It listened to the sound as the men maneuvered their vehicles toward the nest. *What are they doing?* It cast its eye upon them and spotted the boy who had gotten away; the one called Billy had come back and brought others with him. It had expected the priest but hadn't given the others much concern. Still ... it was ready for them.

It called out to the serpents once again. Their bodies, still useful and not yet spent, had more than enough strength left to deal with the nuisance and protect the brood while they rested. It unleashed them on the men, knowing if any of the intruders were to find their way inside, there was still something waiting for them. Something that worked even faster than snake venom; something the priest had tasted firsthand.

The door to the shed flung open, and the three children were tossed inside onto the dirty wooden floor. Troy came down hard on his hands and knees, landing face-to-face with one of the creatures. It opened its eyes and focused on him with intent. A scream stalled in Troy's throat with the black pupils of the creature fixating on his own. Though they were much different than the last time he saw them, the eyes were still familiar. The face and the body had changed greatly as well, but there was no mistaking the thing that lay before him.

He tried to back away but couldn't move and remained on his hands and knees staring into the horribly disfigured face. The creature's eyes grew wide as if with recognition, then a single dark tear pooled in the corner of one and ran down the beast's cheek.

"Rob," Troy sobbed. "I'm sorry."

The creature that had once been a fourth grade boy who loved to look for arrowheads in the woods and build haunted houses with his best friend opened its mouth and hissed. "Troooyyy."

It had destroyed everything the child had been. His body contorted into something almost reptilian, with his arms and legs curled up underneath him like a frog. His flesh was a pallid greenish-grey and looked more like leather than skin. Folds of loose canvas, too big to cover the shrunken body, hung like flaps of stretched-out rubber. Troy fixated on the dark streak as it crawled down the creature's face. It clung as a single drop from his old friend's chin before falling onto the floor. A memory from what could have been another life flashed for a moment, then was gone. A group of children separated from their mothers for the first time, and the comforting reassurance of one boy … Robert Boyle, and one single tear.

"Troooyyy," it hissed again, a tendril of smoke lifting out from between the creature's jaws. Unable to move, Troy watched as more of the strange substance rose from the thing's mouth and began to swirl in the air before him like a cyclone. From somewhere inside the shed, he could hear Wendy and Dawn screaming, but he was paralyzed. The swirling mass was hypnotic and made him dizzy, and he was unable to look away. It wrapped around itself, growing dark and then grey, then a mixture of the two. Troy gasped at the sight of the apparition as his eyes grew heavy.

It rushed at him like a bullet and forced itself upon him. Troy felt the icy gust fill his mouth and enter his windpipe. Before he could think, it was in his lungs and took hold of him. He sensed the satisfaction felt by the presence and watched as the monster rifled through his memories. He fought to push the invader out of his head, and it bit back. Troy collapsed against the old wooden floor as the beast stole his breath. Everything he knew, all he had ever witnessed was there for the taking; the creature sifted and ransacked and consumed what it wanted. It was eager and it was hungry. It also had no idea that Troy was still there, watching from somewhere in the darkness.

While the Rob-creature transferred its presence into Troy, a similar transfer was occurring just a few feet away. Dawn was overcome when the dark cloud left Ben Richards, and Wendy succumbed to what had resided in its twin sister, Erin. The sudden and immediate transition of the Entity's presence was fast and consuming. Neither of the girls' bodies were able to handle the onslaught of genetic information.

Wendy collapsed and started to convulse, the fever ripping through her frail body. It bore deep into her mind and attempted to take control of the child at once. But it never worked that way with the little ones; theirs was a slow burn as their malleable defenses fought off the invasion. In its lust for power and need to satiate its hunger, it had tried to consume her completely. It eased back its grip on the child. But their resistance would only last so long; it was a process they needed to go through and the reason it had first appeared as an infection—or flu, as the doctors labeled it. Its greatest disguise was how it could manifest as a sickness, which was always dismissed, until the children grew weak and its control became omnipotent.

Dawn radiated heat like an inferno and had also begun to tremble. The Entity relaxed its grip on her as well. It would have to wait to settle into its new hosts. Which wasn't anything new, it had waited many times in the past ... it was good at waiting.

It watched through the eyes of the protectors, the ones who had delivered the children. The old hosts were already losing cohesion. The one called Rob fell against the floorboards; darkness ran from its eyes and mouth, where it pooled around the body, then disappeared through the cracks. Erin and Ben ceased to move as well. The female's head smacked against the hard wood. Her dark eyes rolled back in her head and turned over white. The essence had left, and her tortured flesh had already begun to liquefy. Her brother went through a similar process as the ether spilled out of him and into Dawn. It was done much like the way a snake shed its skin; the spent bodies of Robert Boyle, Erin Richards, and her twin brother, Ben, were no longer viable. They would remain where they had been discarded, a combination of myriad creatures from multiple time periods: part human, part reptilian ... all monster.

The heavy rain from yesterday's storm eroded much of the loose gravel from the surface of the old road and gullied out many of the existing crevasses even further, leaving huge potholes and craters that made navigating the bikes difficult. Ted nearly wiped out a dozen times and was almost sent over the handlebars when his front tire caught in one of the larger cracks. Now that they were making their way down the slope and back to the truck, it was noticeable just how dangerous the old pavement had become. With the added threat of their pursuers, the need to remain upright on two wheels was paramount. Ted eased back on the throttle and applied the brake.

Billy, who wasn't nearly as daring as he had been on the way up, followed Ted's lead and descended the hill at a steady pace. By the time they reached the truck, Brandon had taken position at the deck gun, while Bob stood at the side manning the controls of the pump.

Ted pulled up to the back of the truck, threw down the kickstand, and jumped off. He headed straight to the side where Bob had set up shop and grabbed one of the hoses. It rolled out easily as Ted headed for the front of the truck and positioned himself near the right bumper. Billy followed close behind and stood at the left side with the other length of hose.

Lifting the visor of his helmet, Ted called out over the roar of the engine: "Okay, we're in position!"

Bob heard him and opened the valves, allowing the pressurized water to rush into both lengths of hose. The inch-and-three-quarter tube filled quickly and tried to jump out of Ted's hands as he reached for the nozzle. He gripped it tighter to compensate for the force of the water.

"Good to go!" Bob yelled from the side of the truck.

Ted checked to see the hose Billy held was fully loaded and the kid was ready to go as well. "We're good," he said, then stared at the crest of the hill with nervous anticipation.

He continued to watch the road for any sign of movement, then turned to Billy and shrugged his shoulders. Billy gave him the universal sign to wait a second. But there was no movement from either side, and nothing showed itself at the top of the old extension.

Ted squinted and struggled to focus on the crest of the rise, which appeared to grow hazy. At first, it was barely noticeable, and he thought he might have dust in his eyes. Then it became clearer, as if the very top of the mountain had started moving. A series of waves began to spread out, looking like the heat vapors that rose from the pavement on sweltering days. Only it wasn't summer, and Ted knew what was headed their way. The waves grew wider and stretched out to cover the entire width of the road. A pulse of movement rippled through the mass as the strange shape began to descend the mountain and make its way toward them.

Ted gripped the nozzle and planted his feet. It was an impossible scenario, but there wasn't much about the past week that wasn't. From what he could see, the kid hadn't been exaggerating at all. It looked as if every snake in the damn state was on that road. The mass of twisting bodies became more visible the closer the creatures encroached on their position. Ted felt his heart beat triple time; a cold sweat streamed down his back, slicking his shirt to his skin. "Okay, Sheriff. It's time," he said under his breath.

Brandon had a much better view of the approaching mass and was able to make out the individual bodies of the deformed reptiles. Something horrible had happened to them, distorting and twisting their once streamlined features. The snakes were still swift and deathly fast, but they had been disfigured. Massive boil-like growths that looked like infections distended their bellies and backs. Many of the reptiles had lost their pigment as well. The heads of the creatures had grown, and it looked like their venom sacs had tripled in size. Some resembled timber rattlers, others could have been coral or kings, but without the typical vibrant marking, it was impossible to tell for sure. Now they all looked similar, one just as lethal as the next.

The young fireman adjusted the elevation of the deck gun with the foul creatures drawing closer to the truck and the men standing in front of it. He tested the traverse, making sure he could sweep the street quickly, and decided he was happy with the movement; he would be able to execute what he had come to do.

The truck's engine was loud, but another noise rose above it. The sound the reptiles emitted made Brandon's skin crawl. The combination of their tortured hissing and the writhing sound of their misshapen bodies slithering against the broken pavement was nauseating. He felt his stomach flip and fought to hold on to his lunch. The creatures snapped and bared their teeth and lifted their heads in the direction of the men. They had closed more than half the distance down the mountain and were now moving faster.

Brandon's hands grew slick, and his mouth went dry. With every nerve heightened, he waited for the mass of creatures to descend the last twenty feet.

"Almost ready!" he called down to Bob.

The chief had primed the pump and adjusted the throttle. As soon as the gun and the two hoses were fully operating, he'd need to watch the controls and adjust them accordingly. The three men would be shooting a hell of a lot of water at once, and that meant Bob would have to stay at the pump and constantly readjust it. If he allowed the RPMs to tack too high, the engine could seize, and if the PSI dipped below sixty, then the hoses wouldn't work. He needed to balance the master as well as the intake pump and the outtake. Every fireman's worst fear was the possibility of a pump becoming air locked, which happened one of two ways: from a loss of pressure or from the hydrant running dry.

Bob readied himself and took hold of the valve that fed the deck gun. As soon as Brandon gave the word, he would let it rip.

"Okay, Chief. Here we go!" Brandon called as the snakes closed the gap "One ... two ... three!"

Bob turned the valve and watched the pressure dip slightly on the main gauge. He adjusted it and listened to the sound of the engine's RPMs speeding up to feed the pump. The hoses began to fire, and Bob knew the fight had begun. He lowered his hand onto the butt of his sidearm, just to make sure it was still there. *So far, so good.* He adjusted the pressure to compensate for the high water volume coursing through the pump. Although he was curious to see what was happening, he didn't dare leave his position; he trusted the other men had it under control.

CHAPTER 99

From where they stood at the back of the old parking lot, the asylum looked dead and forgotten; if Don had to guess, he would have said it was empty. And he would have been wrong to do so; the place was the delineation of death, but it was far from empty. Although presently inactive, the massive hive that clustered in the basement was very much there. Carl checked his watch and nodded to Stephanie and Don that it was time.

Don set the packs on the ground before him, then pulled on the thick gloves with the rubber palms and extracted a set for Carl and one for Stephanie.

"You'll need these." He handed the pair to the sheriff, who looked at them and grimaced.

"I don't think these will protect me if this stuff goes off."

"You didn't use much dynamite in the war, did you?" Don asked Carl, who shook his head and shrugged. "I didn't think so. Trust me on this. You really want to wear these when you handle dynamite."

The sheriff accepted the gloves, and both he and Stephanie pulled them on. Don unzipped the first bag, revealing an obscene amount of explosives. He had taken the time at the quarry to band the sticks into tightly wrapped bundles of ten. Two wires extended from the center of the bundles where the blasting caps had been inserted. At the other end of the wires were the timers, which were nothing more than fancy stopwatches.

Don removed the rest of the bundles from the bags, eight in total, and carefully turned back the timers to the twenty-minute mark.

"That should give us more than enough time to set them and get back here. We need to be long gone before this stuff goes off, so I'm going to give you two stacks each. Are you sure you're both ready for this?"

Stephanie offered a thumbs-up, and Carl nodded in affirmation.

Don focused on Carl, the way his hands had started to shake and the strained look in his eyes. The guy probably hadn't slept in days. "Are you sure you're up to this?" he asked again. "Because you don't look so good."

"I'm fine!" Carl snapped. "I'll be better when this is over and I can get some sleep."

Don nodded. Of course, that was it. The sheriff had been pushed to the limit since last weekend and probably hadn't eaten in over a day as well. "Okay. Whatever you do, you don't want to drop this shit; it will seriously ruin your day."

Stephanie counted the eight stacks lying before them. "If we each get two, then that leaves you with four to set. That place is huge. Are you insane?" She furrowed her brow and stared back at Don.

"I'll go around the right side, then head to the rear of the building. I'll backtrack and set the charges as I go. I want you," he told Carl, "to hit the left side and set these in the shell of the basement windows." Then turning to Stephanie: "You get the front. You see the small windows cut into the foundation on either side of the entrance?"

She nodded, examining the low-set windows.

"All you need to do is place the stack on the sill. As long as you get it close to the mark, there's enough TNT to topple this sucker like the tower of Babel."

Stephanie's face turned red. "You gave me the easy job 'cause I'm a girl!"

"Trust me," Don said. "There's nothing easy when it comes to dynamite. A million things could go wrong ... That goes for all of us."

"Okay ... you're the boss." Carl said.

Don felt the heavy medallion pressing against his chest and hoped it was enough to keep their actions concealed until they were far enough away. He set the last timer and checked his watch. "Okay, here we go." He pressed all the buttons, and the second hands began to tick down. He placed two bundles in one of the bags, two in the other, and handed them to Stephanie and Carl. Then he transferred the four bundles into his backpack and cinched it over his shoulders. "Let's do this."

Don was the first to emerge from the tree line and into the parking lot of the old hospital. Carl and Stephanie followed behind with their packages in hand.

The hulking behemoth stretched out before them, towering over the property like a monolith. The fact it had been allowed to remain at the top of the extension for so long was a mystery. Surely someone owned the property with all its counted sorrows. For whatever reason, it had been left to rot for decades. However, its time of standing sentinel at the top of Garrett Mountain was nearly at an end. Don had never stepped foot in the old sanatorium like most of the people from town; he had never partied on the grounds with his friends and had never made out with a girl at the top of Mountain Ave. But he had heard stories about the place, most of them told by his nephews, Billy and Eric. Now that he had gotten his first look at the Mountainside Sanatorium and felt the presence of the place firsthand, he was glad he had never come here. Don imagined the place had been haunted long before Stephanie's Entity had come to live here. And he didn't even believe in that stuff.

It was more than just the way the structure had been left to rot that made it look evil. Don sensed it in the very ground itself. He scanned the stonework that had crumbled and crashed to the pavement in front of the foundation. Some brave fortune seeker had climbed onto the roof and removed every copper drainpipe and gutter. A bright red heart had been spray-painted across the brick front of the building, bearing the inscription: Mark loves Lizzy. *Sorry, Mark. Looks like I'm gonna be messing up your artwork. I'm sure Lizzy will understand.*

The trio made their way across the torn-up pavement at a slow but steady pace with their hearts racing like Andretti behind the wheel. The blacktop had been overtaken by nature; large trees pushed their way up through the crumbled asphalt. Weeds and scrub brush stood nearly as tall as Stephanie and came up to Don's shoulders. They walked side-by-side and drew closer to the monstrous structure. The sound of thunder rose from the base of the road at the far left of the parking lot. There was another sound even louder than the revving of the engines and the roar of the hoses. Stephanie looked to the men; her eyes widened as the sound of a thousand snakes cried out as one.

Carl squinted; the nauseating sound penetrated his skull, and he swayed for a moment. The sensation passed; still, the chronic gasp of the serpents was an assault to the group's senses. None of them could imagine what the men on the truck were going through.

The cries continued and the roar of the truck grew louder until the trio found themselves standing at the front of the building. No one knew if the medallions Stephanie had given them were helping, but so far, nothing had come after them. They nodded to one another, preparing to set off in separate directions, when the sounds from the road suddenly changed. The high throttled thrum of the engine tacked out, and the cry of the serpents intensified as well. Their screams were now more visceral, as if they had begun to howl.

"God, something's wrong," Carl said under his breath. He turned to the others, who were already looking at him, shocked and terrified.

"We need to move now!" he shouted. "If something went wrong with the truck, we've got a lot less than twenty minutes!"

Don ran toward the right side of the building while Stephanie proceeded to the front. Carl sprang to action and headed in his assigned direction. "Christ, Bob," he cursed over the growl of the serpents. "Watch your ass!"

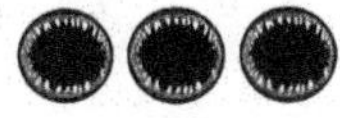

The chief opened the valve, and eighty pounds of pressurized water raced through the line. It entered the deck gun and exploded out of the nozzle in a tight, focused jet. Brandon adjusted the elevation and lowered the pitch of the spray onto the forward line of the encroaching horde. The concentrated water first pounded the pavement in front of the tangle of serpents and then centered on them. The violent power of the jet ripped into the bodies of the creatures, and the water tore them apart. Brandon cranked the traverse adjustment, sweeping the jet across the beasts; a fantail of crimson lifted into the air. Body fluids and pieces of the creatures were thrown across the pavement as if they had been hit by a cannon. Brandon swept the traverse back to the left, releasing another five-foot section of serpents from their mortal coils.

The deck gun was more than effective, making quick work of the serpents that had already closed in on the men. Ted and Billy watched the carnage as Brandon unleashed the initial defensive, then opened the nozzles of their own highly pressurized hoses and pounded the snakes from a lower angle. The combined effort of three jet streams was devastating. Heads, tails, and intestines were thrown in every direction, but mostly back the way they had come. A river of red cascaded down the hill and ran between Ted's boots; a still-rattling tail floated past him and continued down the old road.

Ted never liked snakes to begin with, had always thought they were evil, but these creatures were something far worse. They had gone through a transformation, and it looked like it didn't go quite as planned. It appeared as if there had been a design in mind, that the Entity had a clear idea of what the snakes should become. It had just been physically beyond the snakes' body structure to carry out. Ted focused his jet directly into the pile of deformities and silenced their horrible cries. The other snakes reacted to their brothers' and sisters' destruction and screamed in response; their mutated snake-like language cut through the roar of the jets like a sickle. It was horrible to listen to, deafening and tragic, and almost made Ted feel sorry for having to destroy them. Almost ... he still didn't like snakes.

Billy knew the snakes would be alerted by the sound of the dirt bikes and sent to intercept them; it was the creature's first line of defense in protecting the sanatorium. He and his friends had first encountered the presence Saturday night, probably before it had assembled its army and made the old hospital its home. They may have even stumbled upon it while it was moving in. It looked like a shadow or a cloud of smoke, nothing near as threatening as the possessed creatures that attacked the medical center or the mutated vipers they now faced.

He mowed through the monsters, sweeping his jet stream from the left to right. It had been his idea to lure the creatures out with the dirt bikes, but the chief had suggested they utilize the pump truck. Directing his nozzle, Billy ripped through a tangle of serpents. He prayed the distraction would give the others enough time to breach the perimeter of the sanatorium but had no idea just how omnipotent the creature might be. Still, judging by the ear-splitting reactions of the beasts, he thought they might have a chance.

He opened the nozzle to full and blasted a manhole-sized section of snakes into hundreds of slithering pieces. Billy screamed, focusing all his hatred, until the tears finally surfaced. He had done his best to hold them back, to stifle his feelings, but the destruction of the serpents intensified his memory of what happened to his family. And the dam let go; the tears fell as if driven by their own pump and high-pressure valve. The back spray from the hose lifted into the air and rained down into the open visor of his helmet, camouflaging his tears, but it did nothing to disguise the way his hands had begun to shake and the tremors that raked through his body. However, there was too much going on for anyone to notice that Billy Tobin had lost control.

Bob dialed up the pressure as the demand for water from the hoses and the deck gun diminished the PSIs to the intake pump. He adjusted the setting with the RPMs racing and watched the pressure slowly climb back to eighty PSI. Snake parts and a shower of gore rained down on him where he stood at the controls. He could see the crest of the mountain, and there didn't appear to be an end to the conga line of serpents headed their way.

Then the unthinkable happened; the pressure in the pump dropped to zero and the RPMs shot through the roof. Bob watched the LDH deflate as water ceased to flow through the large-diameter hose.

"Jesus Christ, no!" he screamed, running to the hydrant. The Siamese connection had gone dry as well, and the men were gunning through the remaining water reserve at an alarming rate. Bob didn't know if the hydrant had dried up or if he was looking at an even worse scenario ... a water hammer.

A second later, the pump lost its prime, becoming air locked, and they were dead in the water. Bob's only hope was that a slow stream of water would return and he would be able to reprime the pump. However, the pressurized water that rushed toward the hydrant directly behind the untimely air pocket hit the ancient plug like a two-ton hammer ... a water hammer.

The old unserviced hydrant had been made of cast iron and was unable to handle the force of the hammer. The Siamese connection exploded from the impact of the pressure while Bob was standing directly over the plug. He was hit in the head by a three-inch shard of cast iron. The metal penetrated his skull, and he fell backward into a river of serpent soup. Bob Jones was dead before his head met the ground; he never saw what hit him.

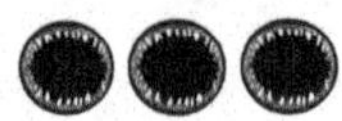

The pump's reserve water supply went dry just before the hydrant erupted. At first, Ted thought the sheriff and the others had begun to set off the charges. Then he saw the huge plume of water jetting into the sky behind him. The hose in his hand went limp, and the others stopped working as well. *What the fuck happened?* But there was no time to wait for an answer; the mass of vipers regrouped and honed in on their position. He turned to

Billy, who twisted and punched at the non-working nozzle in his hands. Ted watched the frantic way that Billy attacked the hose and could see the tremors raking throughout his body. He rushed to his side and yanked the hose from his hands.

"That's it. The pump is dead!" he screamed over the erupting flow of water and the shrill cry of the snakes. Ted grabbed him by the front of his jacket and shook. "We have to move, now!"

Billy looked up at him as if in a trance. "What?"

Ted seized the boy and dragged him around the side of the truck; they stopped short at the sight of the chief's body lying near the shattered hydrant. "No," Ted groaned, and approached the man who had been operating the pump. He looked down into the chief's open eyes; a portion of the man's skull was missing.

"Nooo!" Brandon screamed from the top of the truck.

"Get down," Ted called up to him. "We've got to get the hell out of here ... now!" He pulled Billy to the back of the truck where they had parked the bikes, unslung the shotgun from his back, and turned it on the horde. The snakes were almost on top of them. Ted fired at the masses, blasting a hole in their line of offense that was filled in by more creatures just as fast. He fired again and jumped when another weapon erupted to his left. Billy Tobin had regained enough of his composure to join the fight. The men continued to blast away at the snakes, with little effect other than a momentary disruption in the creatures' momentum.

"Get down here, Brandon!" Ted called, but the boy was nowhere in sight.

The serpents reached the front wheels of the pumper and made their way closer to the back tires; still, there was no sign of Brandon. Ted called to him a third time and was alerted by the sound of gunfire from the front of the vehicle. The kid had moved toward the cab and decided to battle the creatures from there.

Ted and Billy exchanged a disheartened look; there was nothing more they could do other than attempt to lead the snakes away from the truck and the sanatorium. The deputy hopped onto his bike and Billy followed. Together, they coasted away from the truck without starting the engines. It took less than twenty seconds to make it halfway down the hill, far enough to reach a safe distance. Ted popped the kickstand and dismounted the bike; he turned toward the truck to see Brandon panicked on the top of the vehicle. Brandon screamed and shot at something that had gotten too close to his feet. Ted turned away, unable to watch anymore. The next sound to leave the young fireman's lips reverberated as if the man had been set on fire; Brandon fell onto his back and screamed for another few seconds, then fell silent.

The snakes accelerated their pursuit and descended the mountain towards the men on the bikes. Billy shot into the parade of bodies, which did little to slow their attack.

"Jesus Christ." Ted scowled, then hopped back on the bike. Billy fired again at the creatures, then followed. They coasted down the hill another thirty feet and turned to shoot at the serpents once again. They repeated the process until they found themselves at the downed fence where Mountain Ave met the access road. The snakes never ceased their pursuit, but from what either men could see, the size of the horde had diminished. Ted and Billy led the rest of the monstrosities away from the sanatorium and the old extension. The diversion had worked, but it had come at a high price.

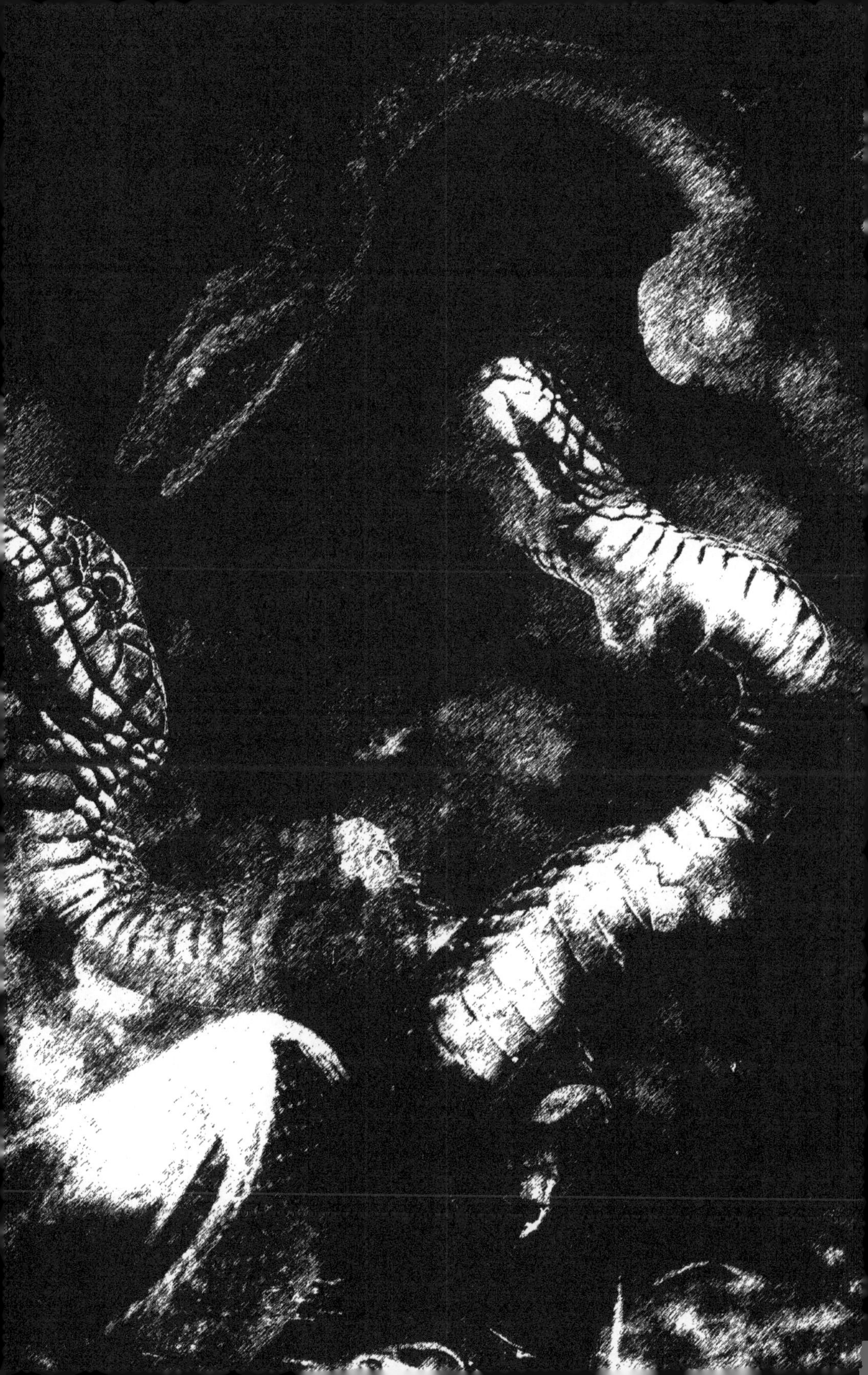

Chapter 100

Don made his way along the far side of the building and heard the horrible grinding noise of the pump when it became air locked. He didn't know what to make of it at first, thinking it was operating under normal conditions. Then the engine raced to an ear-splitting decibel, followed by the sound of an explosion. He jumped when the hydrant erupted and almost fell with the backpack of dynamite.

The landscape surrounding the sanatorium hadn't been tended to in decades, making it near impossible to wade through the chest-high tangle of weeds and scrub brush. Tightly knit vines wove throughout the property and across the face of the structure. It took Don three full minutes to navigate the right side of the building, and by the time he reached the back, nearly seven had passed. He had allowed more than enough time for Carl and Stephanie to set their charges but realized now that he would be cutting it far too close himself.

He quickened his pace as much as he dared and trudged through the overgrown weeds. Large thorns slowed his every step; Don winced as their barbs dug into his legs and tore at his jeans. Still, he forced himself to continue onward.

It took another minute to reach the furthest window in the back. He bent down to the glassless frame and was overcome by the most oppressive stench he had ever encountered. The rancid odor of death rose from the basement and smacked him in the face. Don gagged and nearly passed out. Biting back the urge to vomit, he set the first bundle of dynamite on the window ledge at the base of the foundation.

He doubled back the way he came, retracing his steps along the back of the building toward the second window. More of the deadly thorns attacked him, penetrating his skin and drawing blood. Don suffered through the pain and approached the next window.

The noxious smell was just as bad; the acrid stench of death now appeared to be everywhere. Don tasted it in his mouth and smelled it on his clothes; the odor of rotting flesh saturated the very ground. He held his breath, reached into the bag, and removed the second bundle of explosives. "Damn," he cursed, looking at the timer. Ten minutes had already passed, leaving him only another ten to set the last of the explosives and make it to safety.

Don placed the charge on the window's ledge and sped off to the right side of the building. He cursed himself for doing so, knowing full well the danger of running with explosives on his back, but the urgency to make up some time was paramount. He convinced himself he was only retracing his steps and felt somewhat confident even though he couldn't see where he was stepping. He reached the corner of the building and banked a hard right. Don picked up the pace, with the next window less than twenty feet away. Then ... his right leg went out from under him. He was thrown off balance as his foot sank into the old gopher hole, his leg disappearing into the dirt up to the knee. Don's upper body continued its forward momentum. The stomach-lurching sound his ankle made when it snapped in the forgotten burrow was consuming, and Don almost passed out.

He fell into the overgrowth with his leg held fast in the ground. Bile rose in the back of Don's throat as the pain blasted through him. He turned and vomited onto the grass, his head spinning as if he were on a carrousel. Consumed by blinding light, Don struggled to figure out what had happened. The confusion passed a heartbeat later, and Don realized with laser clarity that he still had twenty sticks of dynamite on his back with the timers set.

He pushed himself onto his hands and one good knee and attempted to lift his injured leg out of the hole. At first, it wouldn't budge; the dirt held fast against his throbbing foot. Don screamed with sweat drenching his forehead and running into his eyes. He gritted his teeth and pushed through the pain, attempting to free himself a second time. The dirt closed around him like a suction cup; then finally, it loosened and partially released its grip. Don's leg shot from the gopher hole, and he fell forward onto his face. White-hot pain blinded his vision, and the world began to go dark. He struggled to remain conscious, but it was too intense. He passed out in the grass with two full bundles of dynamite strapped to his back and less than seven minutes left.

Carl knelt to set the first bundle of explosives at the base of the foundation and hesitated. The changing volume of the pump engine caused him to turn toward the road. The motor's racing RPMs accelerated to a lunatic speed, then halted. Less than a full second later, the hydrant blew. Carl jumped and nearly dropped the ten sticks of dynamite through the open window into the basement below. His heart hammered in time with the rapid concussion of gunfire that followed. *Dear God ... no!* Something had gone terribly wrong, but his thoughts were drowned out when the battalion of serpents screeched as one.

The sound of weapons fire meant the men were still alive, but things hadn't gone as planned. Best-case scenario, the men could still hold off the invading army, but there were too many variables. *Shit!* Carl turned back toward the window and leaned in closer to set the package on the sill. That's when it hit him.

The foul stench rose from the basement and sucker punched him. It was the rancid smell of death with an underlying stink that Carl found far too familiar. The paralyzing funk of rotting fish filled his sinuses, causing him to freeze. It rushed at him like a predator and thrust him back in time, back to that day on the Delta. Olfactory recall kicked in as the scene replayed itself over again on the canvas of his psyche.

Carl found himself waist deep in the brackish waters of the Delta. Thousands of rotting fish covered the surface, putrefying in the Asian sun. He watched the chopper as it lifted into the air and then headed toward the horizon. Wiping the sweat from his brow and doing his best to keep his weapon out of the water, Carl turned and pushed forward through the gravy of dead fish and swarming haze of black flies.

The banks of the Delta lay before them, peppered with endless fields of rice paddies. Tall grasses swayed against a breeze that did nothing to diminish the oppressive heat. Carl looked back and nodded to his platoon—Hacksaw and Tank, followed by Tennessee and Tucson; the Sarge was sandwiched between Big Joe and Little Joe, leaving Goober and Ralph bringing up the rear. Carl locked eyes with Ralph, his only real friend in this God-forsaken country. The big guy had a girl waiting for him back home, and Kerri Ann was expecting their first child.

Carl froze, the sirens in his gut screaming at him. He opened his mouth to warn Ralph; it was on the tip of his lips, but his heart twisted in his chest before he could react. He knew about the landmine and that Ralph was about to step on it; still ... panic paralyzed him, and he couldn't form the words. The only thing Carl could focus on was the overpowering stench of the fish. His hands shook as the scene replayed itself in his mind's eye. *For God's sake, Ralph. Don't Move!* But he could only watch as the platoon proceeded forward, making their way closer to the shoreline. The corpses of the fish increased in density and mass and the all-consuming odor. *Dear God ... the horrible stench of fish.*

Ralph locked eyes with him and smiled. Suddenly, all other emotions were stripped away. His eyes bulged as terror rearranged his features. He knew he had stepped on it; the click echoed beneath his boot and resonated through the water to where the other men stood. Ralph opened his mouth to scream; "Loo—" was all he got out before the water erupted like a geyser.

A tidal wave of crimson washed over Carl. A baptism of pulverized fish guts marinated in Ralph's blood rained down. It entered his mouth, covered his face, and ran into his eyes. Carl felt the scream forming in his throat, but before he could release it, the scene began to fade. It was replaced by a familiar sensation in his gut. *Something's wrong ... something is very, very wrong.* He was catapulted back into the moment by the sound of someone calling his name.

"Carl!"

Every muscle in his body went rigid. Sweat poured from his brow and his hands shook as he looked around to locate the owner of the voice but found no one there. The memory of the Delta faded to a whisper, and Carl regained a sliver of his composure, realizing he had succumbed to another flashback. He stared down at the stack of dynamite in his hands. Over five minutes had passed with less than seven left until detonation. His gut twisted and spoke up once again; something was terribly wrong, much more than just what was happening with the men on the truck. He was sure someone had called his name and could almost recognize the voice as that, too, faded with the Delta.

He set the dynamite on the ledge, turned back the way he had come, and headed to the next window. Holding his breath, he placed the second bundle in the appropriate crook at the base of the foundation, then ran toward the front of the building. Carl hit the corner like a bat out of Hell to find Stephanie standing in the parking lot facing him. She lifted her arms and shrugged her shoulders. He quickly closed the distance with sweat plastering his hair to his forehead.

"What happened to you?" she asked. "You look like hell."

"It's a long story. Where's Don?" Carl looked at the far side of the building to find no sign of movement in that direction. He suddenly realized why his gut had called out so urgently. "Jesus Christ!" he cried. "Something's wrong!"

Stephanie took off after him the second he started running and followed across the busted blacktop of the parking lot. "Please, God, please, God," she chanted, with Carl leading the way.

They found Don's trail immediately and retraced his steps though the tall grass. Carl glanced at the windows lining the foundation and noticed that none of the charges had been set. *This is bad. Where the fuck are you, Don?*

The grass was taller on this side of the building and riddled with gopher holes. Carl spotted them right away and navigated a wide berth. They approached the far corner of the building when Carl noticed the mass of camouflage sprawled out in the grass. It was Don, his body laid out face first. "Christ. No!" he shouted and rushed to where the man lay.

Stephanie gasped as she approached and knelt down beside him. Don groaned and attempted to lift himself off the ground but couldn't right himself. His right ankle remained partially lodged in one of the numerous gopher holes, and it was evident what had happened.

She lifted his head and slapped him across the face. Don's eyes opened at once.

"What?" He blinked as terror flooded his features. "The dynamite!"

Carl removed the pack from Don's back and opened it; there were three minutes left on the timers. He reached in and removed the two remaining bundles, the thick rubber gloves he wore causing him to fumble for a moment. He looked down the side of the building and moved to set the last charges.

"No." Stephanie stopped him. "Give them to me. I'll never be able to lift him; you have to carry him out of here."

Carl held on to the explosives and stared back at her, knowing she was right. The woman was five foot one, two at the most, and there was no way she could move Don by herself. He would have to carry him while she set the last of the charges. It was the only way. He handed her the bundles and nodded to the side of the building.

"Set that shit and get the hell out of there!" he barked, then bent down and hefted the injured man over his shoulder in one lift. Don screamed when Carl grabbed him and started moving.

He stumbled, then Carl shifted and compensated for Don's full body weight on top of him. He started to run, slow at first, then fell into a decent stride. He continued as fast as he could, avoiding the minefield of gopher holes that now revealed themselves to be everywhere. He jumped over one and nearly landed in another, all the while wondering how Don had made it as far as he did without breaking his leg sooner.

Stephanie watched the men retreat toward the front of the building with a stack of dynamite in each of her hands. She looked down at the timers ...

She had less than two minutes left.

Its divided essence rested within the three new hosts. The children lay on the floor of the shed unconscious and sick. Sweat drained from their bodies as the ether pushed to accelerate the becoming process. But the harder it forced its intrusion, the worse it affected the children, their systems threatening to shut down as it sought to consume them faster than it knew possible.

It had been hyper-focused on the acquisition of the three and neglected what was happening on the mountain. It sent its eye into the vipers and watched them advance on the two remaining men. The controllable reptiles made an effective line of defense but weren't built for evolution and had almost been destroyed in the becoming process. However, their venom was more than just toxic; it was like nothing this era had ever seen.

Alarms sounded within its sensory awareness. It couldn't see what was happening but knew something was very wrong. It attempted to zero in but was unable. Rage filled its consciousness with the realization that there was an additional threat to the hive. It wasn't possible; it had left the mind trap for anything that might slip past the vipers. Nothing living could evade it, and its flawless nature had worked perfectly against the priest's group. Still, the threat was there, and it was dangerously close to the hive.

It was still too early, and it had risked much by sending the Butchie-creature out into the light. The protector's body was already showing signs of deterioration, but there was no other option. It focused its projected eye from the shed and directed it on the hive. Still, it couldn't see the threat. This had never happened before.

An echo stirred within the presence ... a memory ... this *had happened* ... once. The beings called Lenape had tricked it. Blinding rage filled its vision; it entered the hive and roused its army from their rest cycle. A glimmer stirred within it, a sense that it was risking a great deal by sending the brood into the light. But it wasn't anything close to rational thought. That was a human quality. The Entity acted on pure bestial instinct.

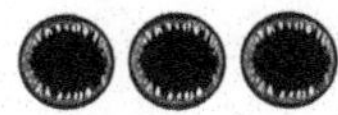

Stephanie ran along the side of the building with her heart in her throat. She sidestepped to avoid one of the massive gopher holes and proceeded to the closest window. The glass had been broken out of the frame decades ago, and as she bent to place the explosives on the sill, the penetrating funk assaulted her like an air strike. It was death ... suffocating ... rotting flesh. The creatures had amassed within the basement by the thousands; their stench was incapacitating.

She gagged and nearly vomited, then she heard the first tortured cries emanating from within. *They're awake! And now they're coming.* The clamor of the beasts as they clawed from their crypt rose in volume. Stephanie listened to the sound of their taloned hands and feet scrambling across the basement floor, and a second later, the world erupted in a chorus of shrieks. *They know I'm here.* The beasts had figured out what they were up to.

She froze for a moment too long, her legs glued to the ground. Looking down at the last remaining bundle of dynamite in her hand she watched the timer pass the one-minute mark, which finally got her moving.

Stephanie raced along the side of the building at a full sprint, her muscles propelling her through the tall grass like a gazelle. It didn't matter that she was short and her legs were small; she had been a ballerina for years. Stephanie's petite dancer's legs pumped like a diesel locomotive. She reached the final window and barely stopped to set the explosive; however, it was long enough for Stephanie to focus on the minute hand as it ticked past the thirty-second mark.

The ghastly sounds erupting from the basement were deafening and frantic. The beasts had mobilized and soon would be exiting the building. Stephanie lowered her head and pushed herself to the point of collapse. It had been years since she exerted her body in such a way, but it came back as familiar practice, and she didn't miss a beat. Her heart raced quicker than the seconds on the detonators, and Stephanie knew she had less than twenty heartbeats left. One missed step, one unfortunate gopher hole, and she'd end up just another stain on the property. She made it to the corner of the building in time to see the distant figures of the men disappear behind the tree line as Carl slipped into the woods with Don on his back. They had made it. But she was still so far away and had so much distance to cover and very little time.

The basement of the old sanatorium had been gutted and left to rot. Several gurneys lay overturned in one of the back corners. Black mold from decades of rainwater seeping in through the broken windows and the no-longer-functioning drainage system coated the floor. And one of the foundation walls had caved in from the excessive rain from yesterday's storm.

Those maladies were the least of the problems that plagued the basement of the old hospital. Now it truly was a place of monsters. Many of which had already started to decompose. Their flesh, pushed beyond its capabilities, could no longer fight the infection. Blood, gore, and non-functioning organs were discarded with every movement of the horde.

At once, they were awakened by the voice. There was trouble, but the directive was obscure. They had always been sent out with clear instructions, but this was different; they had simply been roused and sent out in a general fashion. The hive reacted to the master's uncertainty and frustration; had they still possessed human emotions, it would have been labeled fear. They responded in kind with cries of rage and aggression. Scrambling to their feet, they clawed up the stairs, pushing past one another to exit the building. There wasn't a single shared concern that they were rushing into the toxic light of day.

They poured onto the first floor, trampling over what had been left of the priest's forces. The hive besieged the front door as the blinding light of day seared their eyes and burned their skin.

Stephanie sailed across the broken asphalt with her legs propelling her into the air like a gold-medal-Olympian. Carl and Don watched the woman from their position. She bolted toward them, clearing half the distance of the parking lot in a matter of seconds. Her feet looked like they never touched the ground as she took flight, pristine and streamlined.

There was movement from just inside the front entrance; something flashed out of the shadows and emerged onto the steps.

"Oh fuck!" Don said as the first beast stared out across the lot and spotted Stephanie. The creature howled, then threw a tangle of arms in front of its face to block out the sun. Behind it, a degradation of fiends followed awkwardly out the front doors.

Stephanie poured on the steam as the first ghoul stepped into the full light of day and shrieked. She spotted Don lying on the ground at the tree line and closed the distance between them. Springing off her back leg, she took to the air, sailing across the final stretch of pavement and coming down in the cool of the woods just as the horde descended the steps of the old hospital.

Seconds later, the air was sucked from their lungs as the front of the building eclipsed before them. The searing light lashed out across the parking lot, accompanied by a concussion that stripped the few remaining leaves from the trees. The detonations went off simultaneously, with the exception of the ones set in the back; those went off perhaps a second or two later, but the effect was the same. The first floor of the building disappeared as the explosion forced the concrete foundation and blockwork outward in a geyser of shrapnel. Fiery red, orange, and yellow flashed, and the exothermic chemical reaction tore the structure apart. What remained of the second and third floors caved into the massive hole created by the explosion. A titanic cloud lifted into the air and rushed across the parking lot at a couple hundred miles per hour. The group buried their heads as dust and debris rained over them and covered the ground where they lay.

The beasts that had started to make their way outside were vaporized by the two bundles that Stephanie had set at the windows on either side of the entrance. Their souls had finally been laid to rest.

It was a long time before Don, Carl, or Stephanie could raise their heads as concrete dust, pulverized building material, vaporized mold spores, and a century of pain clouded the air. It permeated every molecule. As they lay there, a strange hush fell over them and resonated in their ringing ears. Something had changed, possibly their luck. But after a tidal wave of sorrow and pain, Stephanie wasn't about to place her faith in something as impermanent as luck. She held her breath and prepared for the next tragedy to befall their dwindling group.

She didn't have to wait long.

CHAPTER 101

Ted and Billy led the snakes away from the sanatorium and a half mile further down Mountain Ave like a pair of Pied Pipers. The serpents followed as the men coasted their bikes down the hill, stopping every several hundred feet to allow the demonic parade to catch up, then repeating the process. It worked like a charm. Ted imagined he could lead them straight to King Lake, where they would all jump off the dock into the water like a bunch of lemmings. They balanced their bikes and waited once again in the center of the road when the top of the mountain erupted like Mt. Vesuvius.

The explosion took the two men by surprise. The concussive *Wha-Woom* popped their ears and resonated in their sinus cavities. It shook the ground beneath their bikes with such force they were nearly thrown off. A mushroom of black and brown vomited into the sky like a rocket as the sanitorium disintegrated. A growing sense of elation welled up inside Ted as he watched the dark plume spread out like a nuclear blast. He turned to Billy, who hooted and pumped his fists into the air. Then something strange happened. The snakes that had been hot on their trail stopped following, as if the explosion had jarred them from their trance. It appeared as if they had forgotten what they were doing. The serpents stopped, paused for a moment, and then dispersed into the woods in every direction.

The men looked at each other, wondering if it was really over, with neither one able to accept the possibility that it might be. Ted removed the radio from his hip and turned it back on. "Sheriff," he said. "We can see your work from here. Looks like you took out half the mountain." He watched the expanding cloud and tried again. "Sheriff, are you there?"

There was silence for a moment, then the radio blared with static and a familiar voice broke through. "Deputy Lutchen," the man shouted. "This is Burt. We have a big problem. Mayor Marceau, Lois Fischer, and the three children never made it to the boats. Günter called, he had to leave without them." The old man's voice was shaken and frantic.

"Where were they last seen?" Ted shouted into the radio.

"At the medical center when they left for the lake. They were in the mayor's station wagon!"

"Okay, Burt. We'll retrace their steps and see if we can find them. Maybe they had an accident or drove off the road."

"I already did that. I've been looking since we got the call. I checked every road between the center and the lake, and there's no sign of them."

Billy leaned in, hanging on the coroner's every word. "Where are you now, Burt?" Ted asked.

"The foothills behind the Boyle house. Carl and I thought there might be a connection back here, and it was the only other spot I could think of."

Ted remembered the morning they found Felix Castillo's body lying in the middle of Foothills Drive and thought what the coroner was saying made sense. The Boyle house bordered the woods and so did the Richards house. If there was a connection, it was very possible that it lay somewhere in the woods behind those residents. Ted let out an exaggerated breath. *This isn't over.* They all thought it would end with the destruction of the sanatorium, but they had missed something. There was still a missing piece of the puzzle somewhere staring them in the face.

"Copy that, Burt." Ted clutched the radio with a growing tremble in his hand. "As soon as I hear from the sheriff, we'll help you find them. We're coming in from the Mountain Ave side and will meet you somewhere in the middle. Have you found anything yet?"

"I came across some tracks. Three of the sets were small, but I wouldn't exactly call them human looking."

"Those could be old tracks."

"Not likely," Burt said. "The storm would have washed them away. These are fresh. There was another set too. Something big was with them ... something really big."

"Okay." Ted swallowed at the lump in his throat. "Don't take any chances, and wait for us before you do anything."

"Copy that. I'll see you when you get here." The coroner ended the transmission.

Ted was about to try the sheriff again when the radio crackled in his hand.

"Deputy Lutchen, come in, Deputy Lutchen." Ted recognized Stephanie Thompson's voice.

"This is Lutchen."

"Deputy Lutchen," her voice was ragged and out of breath. "We need your help; it's an emergency!" The radio went silent. A cold sweat broke out on Ted's forehead. He turned to Billy, who reacted and jumped down on the kickstart of his bike. A second later, the YZ roared to life with Billy

Tobin gunning the throttle and the back tire smoking against the pavement as he tore back up the mountain.

Stephanie raised her head and squinted against the fine particles still lingering in the air. She coughed, shaking off a layer of filth as she got to her feet and attempted to regain her bearings. The breeze on top of the mountain had picked up and already begun to carry the massive dust cloud away. Its foggy billows tumbled across the parking lot and were sent toppling over the south side of Garrett Mountain in the direction of the quarry. She stared down at the two men, who were both covered in pulverized stone from head to foot.

Don spat onto the ground in front of him. "Am I dead?" He tried to get up and was instantly reminded of his injury with a sharp stabbing pain. He howled and fell back to the ground.

"Easy does it," Carl said, then helped prop him up against a large boulder. "It looks like you broke something."

Don leaned back, braced himself, and attempted to flex the ankle in question. He turned it to the right and left, then tried to wiggle his toes. "Hurts like a bitch, but I can still move it a little."

Stephanie knelt in front of him and slowly rolled up his pants. She gasped; Don's leg had already swelled to almost twice its normal width and turned a deep purple.

"Jesus. That's not good."

"I don't think it's broken," he said, moving his toes with a bit more success.

Carl shook the dust out of his hair, removed the rubber gloves from his hands, and threw them on the ground. There was a metallic *chunk* as they landed on something half buried in the silt. A glint of gold caught the sun and reflected back at them.

"What's that?" Stephanie leaned over and sifted through the mess. She lifted it by the chain; a fine layer of dust fell from the medallion. "Did you drop this?" She looked up at Carl.

"I guess so," he said, patting his chest. "Probably came off when I hit the ground." He reached for the pendant and froze with his arm outstretched. His fingers started to tremble, just slightly at first. Then his face twisted as the tremors took hold of his hand and escalated.

"Ahhh!" Carl grabbed his temples and fell to his knees. Clutching his head with his trembling hands, he continued to cry out as Stephanie rushed to his side and took him by the shoulders.

"What is it? What's wrong?" She bent over the man as he rocked back and forth on his knees. Don focused on Carl and watched with growing concern.

The fit lasted for a minute or more before it finally passed, and Carl's body relaxed. He placed his hands on the ground and raised his head. Sweat poured from his brow and coated his face.

"It's the headaches?" Don stared at him from his position against the rock.

"Y-y-yeah," Carl answered with a waver in his voice. "Christ."

"You used RTD instead of dynamite in Vietnam ... right? Came as a rubber you could mold and handle?" Don pressed.

"What?"

"I don't see what you're getting at," Stephanie said, glancing at the medallion in her hand.

"Yeah. What's with all the questions?" Carl's eyes narrowed.

"You're nitro-sick, Carl," Don stated. "It happens when you touch dynamite without gloves. The nitroglycerine seeps into your pores and gets into your bloodstream. Symptoms include a drop in blood pressure, shakes, and severe headaches." Don shifted against the rock as Carl stared at him.

"He was wearing the gloves," Stephanie said. "You saw him take them off."

"Not today," Don insisted. "The other night, when you took the explosives from my trailer and used them to blow up the Sunset Pass and the Gables Bridge." Don forced himself to his feet and limped closer to Stephanie. She took his hand, and together, they backed away from the sheriff.

"What in God's name are you talking about, Fischer?" Carl barked. "Are you out of your damn mind?"

"I thought I was. But there were two sets of prints at the shed. One belonged to a big son of a bitch, but the others looked an awful lot like those cowboy boots you're wearing."

Carl's face twisted as Don continued.

"I figured it had to be someone who knew a little about explosives. But you'd never used dynamite and didn't know you needed gloves to handle it. It got into your head, Carl ... and you never even knew it was there!"

Carl clenched his fist and gritted his teeth; he stared at the ground in front of him with his breath growing heavy in his chest. "Th-that's not p-possible!" he said as his vision blurred and the image filled his head.

Carl found himself staring down at the trunk of a car that was being loaded by a pair of busy hands. He forced himself to focus against the throbbing in his head and tune into the image more clearly. Boxes were being placed onto dark carpeting that was so familiar it jumped out at him. The trunk belonged to

one of the sheriff's cruisers. The haze lifted, and the dream came back to him fully; there was writing on each of the boxes that read: Danger Explosives. Carl bit back the pain as it tore into him even deeper. When had he dreamt that? He wondered if it had been last night at the armory but knew it wasn't. Possibly the night before.

The view of the trunk faded, and Carl found himself looking at a dusty patch of ground. His eyes came to rest on the top of the old cowboy boots; they were his own. But someone else was there too, another set of boots, torn and much larger than his. They were ripped at the side stitching; the feet within them had pushed through the leather and broken the laces. His view shifted upward to examine the owner of the massive boots. The remnants of the man's clothing hung in tattered rags and barely covered his calves and thighs. Skin that had been stretched to its absolute limit ruptured from the grotesque muscles and veins bulging beneath the surface.

Carl's heart twisted as he recalled the minute details of the dream. The man's torso was bare, covered in thick scales that resembled armor. He followed the vision upward and focused on the face that was almost too deformed to look at. The creature's forehead protruded, and its eyes were as black as coal, but there was something about it that was very familiar. Christ! *Carl thought,* it's that psychopath Butchie Post.

The beast reached into the shed, pulled out two handfuls of the dynamite, and handed it to him. Carl watched his own bare hands accept the explosives and then place them into the trunk of the cruiser… his cruiser. He tucked them into a box that held several timers, blasting caps, and even more dynamite.

Carl shook his head and tried to force the vision out of his mind. He clenched his fists and pressed them against his temples. *What's happening?* The pain erupted like a volcano, and Stephanie rushed to his side once again.

As Carl tried to fight off the headache, another vision crept into view and started to play out.

He watched his own hands take one of the timers, the same type he had used in Vietnam, and connect it to the two leads of the blasting cap. He then inserted the cap into a bundle of dynamite and placed it into the box with the others he had fashioned. He had made four complete stacks.

"Get away from him!" Don yelled to Stephanie.

She looked back at him through a wash of confusion.

"I said, get away from him!" Don screamed, but it was too late.

Carl's head shot back as if it were on hinges, and he zeroed in on Stephanie with a visceral intent.

It had nearly gotten into the sheriff's head the night at the morgue. Rainey had succumbed easily, and it would have taken Carl if it hadn't been for Ziegler. Still, it had tasted the man, and that was all it needed to follow his trail and wear him down. Carl had felt off for the past few days as the presence nibbled away at his defenses, attempting to get inside and control his actions. Some were easier to control than others, and Carl had been a tough nut to crack. But the man had pushed himself to the point of exhaustion, which had ultimately worked against him.

Wednesday night, after the fires at the medical center and gas station, the sheriff was close to collapsing. That's when it latched on to him and turned him into a weapon. Carl believed he had gone home and straight to sleep. Instead, he had driven to the quarry, where he met with the recently assimilated Butchie Post, Gary Forsyth, and Mandy Griggs. He had backed his cruiser up to the explosives shed that Butchie and the others had broken into.

The Entity had learned what Carl knew about explosives, but its children no longer possessed the finesse to construct such a device. Not only did it need Carl's knowledge but his fingers as well. The sheriff manufactured the weapons, then gave the stacks to Butchie, Gary, and the others. He explained where to place them underneath the bridge and in the cliff face over the pass, then he showed them how to press the button. The creatures waited until just before sunrise to initiate the countdown sequence. By then, Carl had driven home and woke up in his own bed an hour later, exhausted but under the assumption he had gotten close to a full night's sleep. But his headaches grew increasingly worse as the nitroglycerin entered his bloodstream and forced his blood pressure to bottom out.

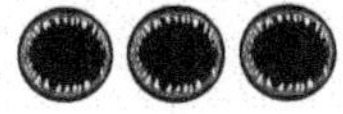

It had sensed something wrong at the nest but been unable to see that Carl and the others were there. It woke its children prematurely from their rest and dispatched them into the light. Then ... pain ... blinding pain ... unlike any it had ever felt before. The nest had been destroyed; all its children silenced at once. Rage consumed it as it struggled to project, but still something blocked its ability to see. Sending its ether out from the shed, it sensed a familiar presence, one it had tasted before. It latched on to the man and looked through his eyes as he stood up and focused on the broken chain lying in the dirt. It scratched at the surface and nibbled away as it attempted to take control of the man once again.

Carl knew it was true; somehow, he had been compromised. It had found a way into his head just as it had gotten into Rainey's. *Christ! I never even suspected.* In a rush of clarity, he understood why he'd always been two steps behind the creature's every move. It had impeded his judgement and affected his decisions from the very beginning. He and Burt had been on its trail, and if they'd only gone back to the foothills, they might have been led back to the sanatorium sooner.

Then he felt it, an itch in the back of his head, impossible to scratch. It gnawed at the base of his skull, twisted like a knife, and entered his brain. The voice was far too familiar.

Carl …

Every muscle in the sheriff's body went rigid. He rose to his feet, balled his hand into a fist, and struck Stephanie under her chin. The small woman was caught off guard and lifted several inches off the ground. Her jaws slammed shut, and her head flew backwards with a violent twist. She landed hard on her back and lay there motionless.

Don lunged to grab him but stumbled on his sprained ankle and fell to the ground. Carl raised his boot and brought it down on Don's shoulder blade. He twisted his heel and drove it deep into the man's back with the full force of his body weight.

Don screamed and struggled to crawl away; he squirmed and scrambled and finally managed to roll over onto his back. Reaching up, he latched on to Carl's boot and attempted to throw him off balance. Don stopped moving when he saw the gun.

Carl pulled back the hammer of the .45 with a shaky hand. Broken blood vessels filled his eyes with crimson as he drew a bead on the man.

“This isn’t you, Sheriff,” Don pleaded to the man inside. “You don’t want to do this.” Don watched the giant barrel focus on the center of his head. There was no use ... Carl Primrose was gone; the beast had taken over.

Now, Carl ...

Carl’s finger tightened on the trigger of the magnum. Like a prisoner trapped within the confines of his own mind, he could only observe as it all played out. The gun steadied in his hand as he took aim at the man on the ground.

Don closed his eyes and raised his hands. He jumped as the concussion of the explosion tore through him like a stroke; he waited for the life to flow out of him. The tremendous weight came down on him and drove the air from his lungs. He struggled to open his eyes one last time, but there was only darkness.

Stephanie stood over the two men, holding the softball-sized rock she had brought down on the back of the sheriff’s head. She threw it to the side and scrambled to pull the man’s dead weight off Don; she grabbed Carl and yanked as hard as she could. The sheriff’s body flopped to the side. She knelt over Don and began to search for the bullet wound; then his eyes shot open, and he exhaled violently.

“Am I dead?” Don screamed.

“No.” Stephanie continued to search with tears streaming down her cheeks. “You’re still here.” She grabbed his face and kissed him.

“What happened?” he asked and tried to sit up.

“I hit him over the head with a rock.”

“What!?! He could have shot me!”

"I didn't have a choice ... You're welcome, by the way."

Carl groaned, rolled over onto his side, and attempted to lift his head.

"No, you don't!" Stephanie jumped to her feet, grabbed the medallion with the broken chain, and quickly tied the two ends together. She looped it over Carl's head and tucked the large pendant under his shirt against his skin.

"My head." He opened his eyes and stared up at the woman. "What happened?"

"I hit you—with a rock!" she shouted. "And I'll do it again if you try anything else. Now give me that radio." She ripped the walkie-talkie from his belt and turned it on. The sound of voices filled the tiny speaker as she bent down to retrieve the .45 lying in the dirt near Carl's side. Then she remembered his second weapon and relieved him of that as well.

"Don't get any ideas," she said, waving the large gun in his direction. "Deputy Lutchen. We need your help; it's an emergency!"

Billy and Ted returned to where they had left the truck and prepared it for evacuation. They moved the bodies of their fallen comrades as respectfully as they could and tucked them into the tall grass at the edge of the pavement. Leaving the scene of the battle behind them, they made their way up the final stretch of the mountain.

"Ugh," Carl moaned, stirring in the backseat. He woke to find his hands bound behind his back and his eyes blindfolded.

Don sat next to him and took Carl by the shoulders. "Easy, Sheriff," he said. "That thing got inside your head. It's probably been there a long time, manipulating you and clouding your judgement." He helped to steady the sheriff as the truck shuddered down the steep mountain.

"What?" Carl asked though a soupy veil of fog. But as Don said the words, the memory came back, and he remembered it all. "What have I done?" he asked, lowering his head.

"It's not your fault, Sheriff," Ted said from his position behind the wheel. "It got to you just like it got to Rainey. How do you feel now? Can you tell if it's still there?"

"Ted!" Carl called out. "Thank God you're here. I don't feel anything but a headache."

Stephanie rubbed the cut on her chin where Carl had punched her. "You're lucky that's all you got. I should have hit you harder."

"I had no idea." Carl shifted in his seat. "It called my name, and then it was like I was watching a movie or something. I heard Don talking about nitro sickness, and then I was there ... at the quarry. Jesus Christ." Carl's voice trembled on the verge of tears. "I made the damn bombs myself. I showed them how to set the timers and where to plant them. I'm responsible ... for all of this!"

"No, Sheriff." Billy Tobin sat on the other side of the man. "You had no control over this. It used you like a weapon; it's responsible for this, not you. It exploits our knowledge, and it could have taken any one of us. It chose you because of the knowledge you possessed."

"I don't feel it anymore," Carl said.

"It got into you when the medallion broke," Stephanie said, turning from the passenger's seat. "They did exactly what I thought they would; the pendants blocked it from seeing us and knowing what we were up to. Now that you're wearing it again, you should be safe ... probably."

"Which means we didn't get it after all; it's still out there," Don added.

"We have another problem." Ted looked back through the rearview. "Um ... Lois and the kids never made it to the boats."

"What!?!" Don and Carl screamed from the backseat.

"Günter Bentley said not everyone had shown up to the boats. When Burt figured out it was Lois, Jessica, and the kids, he went out looking for them but hasn't been able to find the mayor's station wagon anywhere."

"Take this goddamn blindfold off me!" Carl shouted, and Billy removed it for him. "Something went wrong. Not all of the creatures were in the sanatorium."

"He's right," Stephanie said. "And it will continue to spread unless we get all of them."

"Every last scrap," Don added under his breath.

"The Entity itself wasn't in the sanatorium. It might have been at one time, but not when we blew it up." Stephanie's eyes grew wide and welled up. "It's after the children. It can't spread without strong hosts."

"That explains the pictures in the cave." Don's face drew dark. "That's why it took Rob and the Richards twins first."

"We have to find them before it's too late," Billy said what they were all thinking. No one dared mention that since the children were already missing, it was likely they were already infected.

The truck turned onto Mountain Ave, with Ted maneuvering around the double-parked vehicles at the base of the old extension. The road twisted and turned as they continued to make their way closer to town, watching for any signs of movement or life.

"Hurry!" Don shouted from the backseat.

"Ted." Carl leaned forward. "Did Burt say anything else?"

"Yeah, he's headed into the foothills, and we're going to meet up with him. Said he was coming in from the Boyle's backyard. I told him we'd park at the Richards place. Son of a b—" Ted leaned his head forward and brought the truck to a halt.

The group stared out the window at the old house. It was in far worse shape than just disrepair and hadn't seen a paintbrush in far too long. The grass in the front lawn was knee high and contained more weeds than anything else. But the state of the place wasn't why Ted stopped the truck. Parked in the driveway was a vehicle with three of its doors wide open.

"I think we found the mayor's station wagon." Ted pulled the truck to the side of the road. "And that's Butchie fucking Post's house!"

Even from their position in the back, Don and Carl could see the tilted head of the woman in the passenger's seat and knew it was Lois. "No," Don gasped.

"God no," Carl moaned in unison.

CHAPTER 102

Burt walked past the two bicycles that Tommy Negal and Jeff Campbell had left in the woods nearly a week ago. There were many things left lying around by the children of Garrett Grove that were never going to get picked up. However, there weren't enough children left to worry about it. In the wake of the storm and destruction, the town had been all but washed off the map. Still, something had survived. Burt followed the strange tracks to where they entered the overgrown backyard. The tall weeds and grasses had been trampled through recently, leaving a defined path that led to an old shed set back on the property.

Something about the run-down wooden structure caused a cramp to settle in Burt's chest like a coronary. It looked evil, a place of poisonous things. Burt had no idea the shed belonged to Butchie Post and was unaware of the horrific acts that had transpired within.

Burt lifted his gun to his chest and took a step forward. The sound of a large vehicle in front of the residence broke the threatening silence. Then the radio on his hip came to life.

"Burt, it's Deputy Lutchen."

Burt grabbed the radio and whispered, "I hear your truck. I'm in back of the house and think I found something. There's an old shed—"

"Don't go in there!" Ted barked through the speaker. "We need you out front. Right now! For God's sake, hurry!"

Stephanie leaned into the backseat and refastened the blindfold around Carl's head.

"Wait." He struggled. "I can help."

"The only thing you can do right now is get in the way," she said, tightening the knot.

The group exited the truck and rushed to the station wagon, leaving Carl in the backseat. Don was the last one to arrive, hobbling along on his sprained ankle.

Stephanie ripped open the passenger's door of the station wagon and looked in on Lois. The woman's skin was grey, and she didn't appear to be breathing. Stephanie looked down and noticed the hypodermic needle sticking out of Lois's thigh. "Oh no," she cried.

Ted forced his way in and searched for a pulse but couldn't find one. He frantically pressed his fingers against Lois's neck as Don screamed from somewhere behind him.

The deputy removed the hypodermic and shouted into his radio. He pulled Lois out of the front seat and laid her down on the driveway. Lifting her arm, Ted searched her neck again, with the others hovering over him. After several seconds, he looked up to them. "I've got a pulse," he said. "It's weak, but she's alive." He checked her forehead for any sign of fever, then lifted her eyelids. There were no telltale indications of the infection;

the woman had either been poisoned or drugged. A flurry of commotion caught his attention as something hurried toward him from the side of the house.

Burt almost knocked Ted off his feet as he pushed past him to get to the woman on the ground. He went straight to work checking Lois's vitals, listening to her breathing, finding her pulse, and then lifting her upper lip and inspecting the color of her gums.

"Is she going to be okay?" Don asked through a cascade of tears.

Ted lifted the hypodermic to his nose and sniffed. He ran back to the station wagon and focused his attention on the front seat. He spotted the two purses that had been left in the car and began to rifle through them. He shouted and emerged from the car with a vial in his hand.

"Morphine! She's been drugged." He held the vial out to Burt.

"Is she going to be all right?" Don demanded.

"Ohhh." Lois's eyes fluttered and opened to slits as she attempted to lift her head. "Wha the heyyy," she slurred.

"She should be fine, Mr. Fischer," Burt said. "But I need to get her back to the center and let Doris take a look at her."

Don knelt beside her. "Lois, where's Troy? Where are the children?"

"The mayorrr ... took them."

"In the backyard." Burt grabbed Ted. "There's something back there. Several sets of prints, by the looks of it. I think that's where you'll find them." Without another word, Billy and Ted tore off around the side of the house with Stephanie following close behind. Don attempted to get to his feet, but Burt stopped him.

"They can handle whatever's back there, I need you to help me with your wife."

Carl worked at the amateur knot used to bind his hands. He tensed his arms and twisted, slipping out of his confines, and then removed his blindfold. The pain in his head had eased slightly, and there appeared to be no sign of the presence on the edge of his periphery, at least not that he could detect.

He looked up in time to watch Stephanie disappear around the side of the house toward the backyard, then he exited the truck, causing Don to stiffen as if reacting to a predator. Carl intercepted the man before he could remove the large gun from his belt.

"Knock it off, already." He snatched the .45 from Don Fischer. A second later, Carl followed the others around the side of the house.

He caught up to Stephanie and ran past her, giving a quick nod. He raised the .45 and took position with Ted, who had already drawn his own weapon. Together, the men approached the shed door with Billy no less than five steps behind.

Carl examined the grass leading to the shed; from what he could tell, there were five sets of prints. He held his breath as he approached the door, placed his hand on the latch, and prepared to rush inside.

Troy waited ... expecting the presence to detect him at any moment. It had slammed into his head like a nail into a two-by-four, then proceeded to ransack his memories and rifle through his consciousness. It was vile and toxic, and now it was inside him. It smelled like sulfur.

The creature was dark, never holding the same shape for long. At times, it was nothing more than a cloud, shimmering and transparent. From where he hid, Troy could see the metallic particles of the creature's makeup. They swirled and spiraled like dust, only this dust had intention. Twilight from an unknown source danced over the creature's mass and reflected into the dim. Flecks of scarlet, amber, and deep purple flashed as the formless shape lumbered across the strange landscape that Troy instinctively knew was the creature's reality.

It moved further from him, making its way across the bareness of the expanse. Then, in slow motion, the beast and the landscape began to take shape and materialize. It took on the form of a giant reptile, more dangerous looking than anything Troy had seen in his schoolbooks. The beast turned and morphed into an insect with dark hairy legs and great fangs. The spider-like creature then altered into the form of a man and then a massive ape. It continued to shift from one form to the next as it maneuvered away from Troy.

Watching from his hiding place, Troy was gripped with a sudden realization; he knew exactly where he was, impossible as it might be. His hands gripped the bars of the cage, the cold steel familiar against his flesh. It was the first room of the haunted house that he and Rob had built. Troy was standing in an exact replica of the cage in his garage—he was back inside Scream in the Dark. Then he noticed his hands on the bars in front of him; his fingers and flesh were transparent. Troy raised a palm to his face and gasped. He could see through it. A pale luster outlined his features, a stark contrast to the landscape and the makeup of the creature. His body appeared somehow illuminated, while the beast's looked dark and dirty. He moved his hand, watching the trail of incandescent light wash across the canvass before him. Troy stepped out from behind the bars of the cage and made his way into the emptiness that stretched out before him.

The creature had moved on, consumed with locating whatever it was thirsting for. The expanse was dark and vast, and there was a depth to it. The air felt heavy, and although it was alien and unfamiliar, Troy didn't feel as scared as he should. *This isn't Earth. At least, not the Earth that I know.*

There was movement; a dark shape dotting the perimeter slowly came into focus and approached. Troy froze as the featureless shape took form and he found himself standing face-to-face with the woman. It was the girl who worked at the diner; her name was Mandy. Troy remembered she had been nice to him; he had always thought she was pretty. But there was nothing pretty about Mandy anymore. Her head hung limp to the side, and her flesh was dark and murky, like the smoke from a fire. She stopped before him, staring in his direction. Except Mandy's eyes were missing. Black hollowed-out sockets fixated on Troy's position and beckoned for him to release her from the torment. Her sorrow was profound, and Troy could feel every ounce of it. The pretty waitress had been ravaged; there was nothing left of her. Mandy placed her hands against her chest and walked away into the darkness. Troy wanted to scream and to rip the hair from out of his head but found it impossible to do either. Instead, he watched Mandy disappear into the abyss ... the beast's abyss.

He turned away from the awful sight only to find Tommy Negal standing before him with his arms outstretched. His old friend stood there pleading, yearning for salvation. But there was none to be found, at least none that Troy could offer. Tommy continued his search and lurched away into the darkness.

Unable to witness any more, Troy shielded his eyes from the onslaught. But the images continued to appear. Children from his class approached and stared in his direction, all possessing the same grey eyeless features as Mandy. They were followed by others whom Troy had never met.

Somehow, they sensed his presence and had come for his help. Then the landscape itself began to take shape. There was a deafening pulse, and Troy found himself standing in the foothills. A moment later, he was in the graveyard of the Lutheran church. Then Troy was on Pine Street, watching his house from the driveway. He was at the toy store, and then he was at the school, standing in the playground where he, Wendy, and Janis had eaten their lunch.

There was another pulse, and Troy found himself running. He sped through the demonic representation of his town without any idea where he was headed. Only this version wasn't his town; this was the creature's existence. By consuming every consciousness, it had constructed a dark prison where it could roam free without fear of the light. The absence of illumination was apparent in the dimness of the void. Troy felt his feet moving as the gaunt, hollowed-out faces flashed before him. Terror seized him; he realized he would never escape this hell, that he would never see the sun again. Troy ran until he found a familiar door and raced toward it. It was constructed of cardboard and wasn't much of a door at all, but it was one he recognized, one he had made himself.

Troy pushed his way through the secret passage until he came to the dead end. He stood up, wrapped his hands around the bars of the cage, and exhaled, feeling his panic subside slightly. The secret comfort of his hideaway filled him with a sense of security. He shifted his position behind the bars and slid his feet across the strange floor. His heart leapt from his chest, causing him to jump, when he knocked into the object with his sneaker. Troy positioned his foot and he waited. Troy was good at waiting.

Lois opened her eyes and looked up to see Don and Burt leaning over her. A dreamy fog glazed her stare; then her eyes widened, and it came back to her in a rush. She grabbed Don by the front of his shirt and struggled to get on her feet.

"Troy!" she screamed.

Don was almost knocked off his one good foot but managed to remain upright when she grabbed him. He and Burt helped her up the rest of the way.

"Where are they?" She wobbled a bit and frantically scanned the driveway. "Where's Troy?"

"The sheriff is searching the backyard now," Don said, trying to steady her. But the action was ineffective, and Lois slipped from his grip and bolted out of the driveway before either he or Burt could lift a hand to prevent her.

Don hobbled after her, assisted by Burt, who grabbed him under the arm, and together, they followed Lois into the backyard.

Carl pressed down on the latch, feeling the clasp disengage. He nodded to Ted and glanced back at Stephanie and Billy, who were only a few steps behind them. He rested his finger on the trigger of his weapon, held his breath, and eased the door inward. The old hinges strained under the stress and let out a strangled squeal. Carl pushed the door further and was bombarded when the oppressive stench rushed at him and struck him in the face. The odor of rotting meat and decay filled the small structure like the funk of a slaughterhouse. Something had died in the shed and been concealed in one of the corners or beneath the floorboards some time ago. A flashback of the Delta threatened to resurface once again, but Carl bit back and managed to fortify his resolve.

Carl noticed the dark brown stains that painted the floor. Then he saw the thick chain bolted into the wood; a steel dog collar with a padlock was attached to the other end. Carl forced himself not to imagine what it had been used for, knowing that Butchie Post had been busy long before the presence entered him. The windows had been boarded up and fortified, making it difficult to see into the back of the structure, which was still bathed in shadows. Carl shielded his mouth and nose from the assaulting odor and allowed the door to open fully inward. Sunlight fell across the floor, revealing the three small figures and the withered remains of the others.

Carl saw the children and prepared to rush in when an ear-shattering shriek erupted from the silence. A tremendous force rushed at the men from the back corner of the small building. It blasted out of the shadows and smacked into Carl and then into Ted. The deputy was thrown into the door like he had been hit by a linebacker. The wind rushed out of him, and he was knocked off his feet before he could aim his weapon. Carl didn't have time to react either as it hit him with the full force of a tornado and sent him flying backward onto the grass. The .45 was thrown from his hand and landed in a tangle of weeds somewhere behind him.

The mayor burst from the shed after crashing through the two officers. The woman's face contorted with rage; a thin cloud of the poisonous

Entity had already begun to lift from her eyes. Billy and Stephanie had enough time to react and managed to raise their weapons. Billy lifted his revolver while Stephanie produced Wendy's wrist rocket. But the mayor rushed at them with the speed of a cheetah and knocked into Stephanie, who was tossed like a ragdoll. The mayor landed on Billy with her arms outstretched.

Billy felt the woman's fingernails dig into his flesh just below the shoulders as she came down on top of him. He howled and tried to fight the creature off but was unable to breathe. The woman was too strong and continued to drive her talons deeper into him. Billy started to lose consciousness. It was the speed in which the woman moved that took them by surprise; her swiftness and strength was that of a freight train and had toppled their defenses. Carl and Ted scrambled to their feet as the mayor began to tear into Billy Tobin.

A darkened mass grew around the creature's head, lifting from her eyes and mouth. It swirled and twisted in the autumn air, the metallic presence reflecting the sunlight like a thousand black diamonds. Billy found himself hypnotized within it, mindless of the pain in his chest. The mayor lifted her head and howled. A magnificent plume of darkness filled the air like an atomic blast. It gathered before her face, then concentrated its attention on Billy. A dagger-like projection focused on the boy, who had precious seconds left before he, too, was consumed. Billy remained transfixed, unable to protect himself; he forced his eyes shut and waited for the inevitable.

Billy jumped as the presence hit him with the concussion of an explosion. The sensation was unlike what he imagined, and he remained fully aware as the world around him erupted. It sounded almost like a gun being fired.

The first bullet hit Jessica Marceau in the temple. It exited the opposite side of her head, taking a lemon-sized piece of her brain with it. The second and third bullets hit her in an equally damaging fashion, but the first one had done the job. The woman fell off Billy Tobin and landed in the grass. The dark cloud dissipated the moment the bullet was introduced to her brain matter. It lifted on the breeze and quickly dispersed.

Billy waited for the end to take him as the pain in his chest returned and intensified. He opened his eyes to find himself face-to-face with the ruined body of the mayor—more than half the woman's head was missing. His vision slowly cleared, and he looked up at the smoking barrel of the gun. The weapon trembled and then wavered in and out of focus. He struggled to bring the shooter's face into view, knowing it had to be either the sheriff or Deputy Lutchen who had saved him. The weapon was lowered, and the beaming face of the coroner appeared. Burt smiled, then wiped the sweat from his brow.

"No fucking way," Billy managed. He lifted his hand and gave Burt a thumbs-up, then passed out in the grass.

Burt rushed to Billy's side, ripped off his own jacket, and pressed it against the boy's wounds. He had little recollection of drawing his weapon or even taking the shot and had acted on reflex alone. Now, looking down on the boy, he wondered if it had been in vain. Billy was losing blood fast, and his face had gone pale grey. Burt's jacket quickly turned scarlet as he pressed it into the boy's wounds.

"I need to get him to the center, or he's not going to make it," Burt shouted and lifted Billy off the ground. He was joined by Stephanie, who grabbed the boy by the other arm. They ran across the lawn and set him into the backseat of the mayor's station wagon before Lois or Don could react. A moment later, the car sped out of the driveway with Burt's foot pressed to the floor.

Ted managed to rise to his feet before Carl. He rushed into the shed and stood over the three children; they had all been infected. He knelt beside Dawn, whose eyes were open but had rolled back in her head. A cloudy dark film covered the whites and swirled within. Heat radiated from the child like an incinerator. Her body convulsed as the Entity ravaged her.

Carl positioned himself between Wendy and Troy, whose conditions were just as dire. Wendy lay bathed in sweat, convulsing with such force her head beat against the floor like a tom-tom. The swirling cloud was visible in the child's eyes as well; the Entity had attached itself completely. He lifted Troy's hand, which was limp, motionless, and blazing hot. Then he leaned over the boy and looked into his eyes.

"Troy, can you hear me?" Carl jumped as the boy latched onto his hand with the force of a snapping turtle. The dark haze in his eyes lifted, and he stopped shaking. He looked up at the sheriff with a wash of realization and opened his mouth to speak. Then, just as quickly, he was gone. The darkness returned, and Troy's eyes rolled back in his head.

"Troy!" Lois screamed as she and Don entered the shed.

They were too late; it was obvious. Troy, Wendy, and Dawn all exhibited the same symptoms Robert Boyle had shown less than a week ago. Lois rushed to her son and took him in her arms.

"Somebody do something!" The sudden shock pushed the residual effects of the morphine to the side. She turned to Don and pleaded, but he was already on the move. She watched as her husband reached into his shirt and removed something from around his neck. He leaned in and slipped the chain over Troy's head, the large medallion coming to rest on the boy's chest. The effect was immediate. Troy stopped convulsing and settled into a steady, rhythmic breathing. Then the child closed his eyes and lay there as if he were only sleeping.

Lois gasped. "How did you know?" She pulled Troy close and rocked him.

Stephanie rushed into the shed with her own medallion in hand. She knelt next to the little girl and slipped the large pendant around Dawn's neck. The second the object contacted her skin, she stopped shivering. The cloud coating her eyes vanished, and she lowered her eyelids.

Stephanie gave Carl a cautionary look as he motioned to remove his own medallion. "Not so fast," she said, lifting the leg of her pants and exposing the weapon strapped to her calf. She pulled it out and slid the magnetite dagger into Carl's belt, making sure the stone pressed against his skin. Stephanie nodded as Carl slipped the medallion off his neck, leaned over Wendy, and slowly laced the chain around the trembling child. The girl stopped shaking, closed her eyes, and settled into a restful sleep.

"We didn't get all of them." Carl let out an exaggerated sigh, his eyes focused on Stephanie.

"It got to the mayor," Stephanie said. "Something we missed. I don't know what, but now it's in the children. I think this is what it was after all along."

Don had seen the murals in the cave and knew the children were the answer as well. There was something they possessed that the creature needed, and the Lenape had used their own as bait. The skeletal remains confirmed that. The children had been left behind before the cave was sealed, and the creature had been trapped with them. Now it was inside Troy and the girls, although momentarily silenced by the medallions.

"These pendants aren't going to work forever, are they?" he asked.

"I doubt it," Stephanie replied. "It's growing inside them. I think it's only a matter of time before it takes them completely. But you said Troy's friends were sick for a while before everything went to hell, which makes me think we might still have a little time." She scanned the faces of the others. "I don't know if it will work, but I have an idea." She turned to Don, who already knew what she was about to say.

"We have to get them into the cave. You said it yourself. There's something about it that can't be explained."

"What about the cave?" Lois looked to her husband with tears in her eyes. "What's in the cave that can save Troy?"

Don shook his head, pushing aside an image of three small skeletons that had surfaced. "It's a geological anomaly," he said. "I can't say with certainty, but it's nothing science has ever recorded before. I'm not even sure it's terrestrial." He watched as Lois's eyes widened.

"I know it sounds crazy, but if there's any chance of saving them, the answer lies in that cave. And we're running out of time."

Lois pulled Troy closer to her chest. "Please," she cried to Stephanie. "Please save them."

"Quickly," Stephanie said, scooping up Dawn and heading into the sunlight. "Follow me."

The darkness of the void was suddenly illuminated. The creature that had lurked in the shadows at the perimeter of Troy's vision shrunk back and hid itself from view. Troy watched as the world in which he visited altered as well. It had been dark and transparent and inhabited by countless numbers of the creature's victims. Scores of Troy's classmates and people he knew from town wandered the desolate landscape. There were animals and beasts that had roamed the planet eons ago, along with numerous civilizations that had been assimilated over the course of Earth's brief history. Tribesmen adorned in animal skins and paint beckoned for salvation. Puritan settlers in dark garments pleaded to be released from their eternal damnation. But Troy was unable to help any of them as he hid behind the bars with their eyeless stares focusing on him.

The world was eclipsed by a blinding illumination that dispelled the dark figures and faded the landscape. White welcoming light filled his new habitat. Troy sensed a familiar presence; an unmistakable one he had known his entire life.

"Mom," he called out. There was no answer, but he knew she was close. He could smell her shampoo as if she were holding him.

The dark mass darted from place to place, panicked and desperate to escape. *You're trapped, just like me.* Troy watched from his confines.

The creature vanished into the distance and emitted the most vile, torturous sound Troy had ever heard in his life. He covered his ears and tried to block it out as each one of the beast's victims cried out together in pain.

CHAPTER 103

Ted steered the pump truck into the main entrance of the quarry, passing several abandoned vehicles and a scattering of bodies. He stepped on the gas as Don pointed toward the ramp that led to the cavern.

Stephanie and Carl sat in the back with Dawn and Wendy cradled in their arms, while Lois and Don sat in the front holding Troy. None of the children had regained consciousness, but occasionally, Troy pulled himself closer to Lois as if he sensed her presence.

Don motioned for Ted to stop at one of the service trailers and opened the door of the truck. The pain in his leg had subsided some since he had wrapped it with the roll of duct tape that Billy had left behind. His tightly bound boot and the calf of his pants leg now acted as a makeshift cast, fastening his ankle in place. He hobbled out of the truck, retrieved a five-gallon gas can, and returned a moment later. The deputy then pulled the truck up the slope, almost to the entrance of the cave, where the generator sat.

"I need to fill the tank!" Don yelled over the roar of the truck.

"I'll take care of that." Ted said, turning off the ignition. "Get the kids inside and do whatever it is you plan on doing." He took the can from Don and headed to the generator while the others exited the truck with the children in tow. The cool air of the cavern wafted out as they made their way inside.

There was ample light in the first chamber, enough to see where they were going. They cautiously made their way into the second area when the generator roared to life, bathing the entire cavern in illumination. The massive murals painted on every wall revealed themselves to their visitors.

"This way," Don yelled before disappearing into the small opening. The darkness on the other side of the small breach was consuming as the others entered inside. Don turned on one of the flashlights, Stephanie followed his lead, then Carl did the same. "For God's sake, be careful. There's a massive drop-off in the middle of the floor. Follow exactly where I go."

No one needed to be told twice; they stayed close behind Don and Stephanie, following the beam of their lights through the darkness until they finally stopped approximately twenty feet inside the chamber.

"What is this?" Lois gasped, her voice shrill and near hysterics. She followed her husband to the stone altar. The remains of a small skeleton lay on top; the body was no larger than that of her own son's. She pulled Troy close to her chest and stepped back. "Are you out of your mind? You're not putting my son on that thing."

"You have to trust me, Lois." Don took her shoulders and stared into her eyes. "The Lenape used their children as bait. That's not what we're doing here."

Stephanie swept her arm across the altar and scattered the bones to the floor, causing the others to jump. Lois watched in horror as the woman laid Dawn onto the stone slab and positioned the medallion in the center of her chest.

Lois shook herself free from her husband's grasp and backed up several steps. Don watched in horror as she neared the ledge.

"Lois!" he screamed. "Don't move another inch. The drop-off is directly behind you."

She didn't listen and took another step, her back foot coming to rest at the very edge.

"Dear God, Lois. Don't move!"

Lois almost stepped back into the abyss but stopped two inches shy from the ledge. She looked down at Troy as his eyes fluttered. He latched on to her as if he had awakened. It was enough time for Don to reach out and pull them back. He spun her around and cast his flashlight into the massive hole in the center of the floor. Lois gaped at the chasm.

"I'm sorry, but you have to trust me," he said as Stephanie and Carl carried Wendy to the second altar. "I have no idea if this is going to work. But if we don't try, we're going to lose him." His words seemed to resonate, and Lois allowed him to lead her around the chasm to the third stone structure. She looked across the massive pit to see Stephanie rake the bones off the slab and watched Carl lay Wendy down.

She turned back as Don cleared the stone, then she placed her son on the slab. Copying what Stephanie had done, Lois fitted the large pendant in the center of Troy's chest, leaned over him, and kissed him on the cheek. He stirred for a moment, and a smile spread out across his face. "I love you, baby," Lois whispered. "Come back to me."

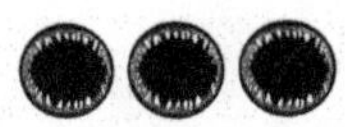

From where he stood, Carl could make out the far side of the chamber, which had been impossible to do when they first entered. He was taken aback by how fast his eyes had adjusted to the overwhelming darkness and watched as the Fischers placed Troy onto the altar. He had no idea what Don or Stephanie expected to take place, but so far, nothing had happened, and he was beginning to think they had come there in vain.

A shadow stepped in front of the entrance to the chamber, eclipsing the light that filtered through the passage. Carl relaxed and watched Ted as he emerged from the secondary chamber, but the deputy had stopped in the doorway and remained there. His body cast in a silhouette with the flood lights shining behind him, his features bathed in shadow and impossible to make out.

"Ted," Carl shouted. "What the hell are you doing? Come inside." He shielded his eyes to focus against the glare but couldn't make him out any clearer.

The deputy took a lumbering step into the chamber. Carl felt the hairs bristle on the back of his neck—something wasn't right. He squinted and shielded his eyes to focus better. It almost looked like Ted had carried something with him at his side, like he was trying to drag it into the chamber. Carl's jaw clenched, and his gut screamed like a siren.

The dark shadow took another step into the chamber and yanked at the baggage it was holding. There was a flurry of movement as something was tossed in their direction. Carl watched as the object cartwheeled through the air and headed directly toward Stephanie. He jumped and pushed her out of the way, knocking her to the ground as the mass landed at their feet in a tangled heap. Carl stared down at Ted's lifeless body. His head had been twisted a hundred and eighty degrees and now faced the wrong way.

"Jesus Christ!" Carl screamed and reached for his weapon, but it was too late. The massive beast slammed into him and seized him by the throat.

The creature that had once been Butchie Post now stood nearly eight feet tall. Its bulbous musculature had ruptured through its flesh. The clothes it had once worn were gone, replaced by scales and a thick layer of coarse hair covering it like an armored primate from some forgotten time.

Carl clutched at the monster's mitts as they wrapped around his neck and clamped down. The Butchie-beast released an ear-splitting shriek as if it were pleased with itself, then lifted Carl and took a step toward the center of the chamber. The sheriff's feet left the ground, and he felt himself propelled backward toward the chasm.

Stephanie regained her footing and quickly removed the wrist rocket from her coat pocket. She dug out a lodestone ball and fitted it into the weapon's pouch. Pulling back on the rubber bands, she let the projectile sail at the massive beast. The projectile missed the creature and bounced off the rock wall somewhere in the distance. She loaded another round into the pouch, drew back on the elastic, and hesitated. The beast dangled the sheriff at the edge of the drop-off; she couldn't risk it. If she hit the creature now, it would only cause it to release its grip on the sheriff. Carl would fall to his death regardless.

Across the pit, Lois and Don were helpless to do a thing when the creature entered the chamber and snatched Carl like a ragdoll. It took him by the throat in a heartbeat and, within seconds, had the man at the edge of the drop. Troy moaned and stirred behind them. Lois turned to her son, who had started to convulse once again. He shook and flailed his arms as if he were fighting the beast himself. She held on to him to prevent him from throwing himself off the narrow pedestal. Don moved to assist her as Troy thrust his arms into the air in a violent series of thrusts and jabs, the first nearly connecting with Don's chin. There was more than one battle going on in the cave, but Don suspected they were one and the same. Troy lifted his arm and clenched his fist. A second later, the beast screamed as if it had been struck.

Ted had just finished emptying the canister into the generator and started the engine when the huge shadow descended on him from the ridgeline above. He was eclipsed in darkness and had just enough time to look up. Then the world that Ted Lutchen knew ceased to exist.

The massive creature had watched the group exit the truck and make their way into the cavern. It didn't want to go anywhere near the rock; it had been fooled once before. But the simple ones had the children, and it could no longer see through their eyes. Something blocked its vision. Rage tore through it like a comet, infuriating every atomic particle of its makeup. It had no choice but to return to the cave and retrieve the children. Then it would ravage the others and make them pay.

It stared through the eyes that had once belonged to a boy named Marion, a boy who had never known his father, one who had experienced a lifetime's worth of abuse from the other children in just a few short years. The memories had festered inside the child and turned him sour. So much so, it had poisoned his very essence. If that hadn't been enough, the continuous rape and beatings endured during his eighteen-month sentence surely had. Butchie Post returned to Garrett Grove far worse than when he left. He had come back tainted, with a hunger for something far more debase.

The shed he kept in the backyard of the house on Mountain Ave was far enough from the road and neighbors that if any of his victims had lived long enough to scream, they would never have been heard. But they were generally at death's door by the time he fastened the dog collar to their necks and the shackles around their wrists. The people who disappeared from Warren and Parker Plains, women and men alike, had never raised the attention of the Garrett Grove Sheriff Department. Butchie had been somewhat disciplined in that regard. However, his appetite had grown stronger as he struggled to sequester his desires. It wasn't enough to incapacitate his victims, it wasn't enough to beat them within a brushstroke of death before he threw them in the trunk of his car, and it wasn't enough to strip and shackle them to the floor of his shed. Butchie's violation continued long after his victims died, and recently he had begun to take notice of the prey within his own community.

It had sensed the predator in the one called Butchie and chosen him for the role of protector; it was as if the boy had been bred for the position.

It stood in the doorway of the third chamber, watching the one called Carl. It had fought to take control of the man and had finally succeeded but was blinded to his thoughts once again. Just as it was to the children. Fury ripped through it when it spotted the little ones on the stone outcroppings. It was reminded of the pain it had felt when the tribal people had lured it inside, a burning within every particle of its essence. It pushed forward, certain that these simple creatures would never sacrifice their children. The one called Ted was now dead, and there was no one left to seal the cave.

But it had been certain before and had found itself trapped just the same. Fury had driven it to the edge, and it had ripped through the Lenape who had been left trapped within the cave. Then it had descended on the children. It tried to turn them but had been far too eager, and something had blocked its reach. With blinding rage, it had forcefully inserted its dominance, and the children had perished.

Now it felt that rage once again; it boiled within as it stood in the doorway of the chamber, watching. It lifted the body of the deputy into the air and threw it across the cavern. The man landed in a broken heap.

CHAPTER 104

Carl stared into the black eyes that had once belonged to Butchie Post and struggled to free himself. But his attempts were futile; the thing was massive and as strong as a bulldozer. It lifted him off his feet and dangled him at the edge of the chasm in the center of the cave. Carl kicked at the beast as it hoisted him into the air and tightened its grip on his windpipe. He felt his throat compress. The air in his lungs turned to fire and started to flame out.

Despite the increasing brightness that had crept into the cave, the perimeter of Carl's vision began to fade as his brain started to shut down. He reached blindly for his weapon only to find it wasn't there, or he was too incapacitated to locate it. He slapped at his hip with his right hand and held on to the monster's claw with his left. His arms grew heavier with each groping motion, and Carl knew it would be over soon. He thrust his hand in a final desperate motion and latched on to it, cold and hard against his belt. Carl's spirit lifted when he realized what was in his grip.

With the last ounce of strength in his reserve, Carl raised the dagger Stephanie had placed in his belt and drove it forward. The tip of the lodestone weapon connected with the creature's chest. A piercing howl erupted as if the monster had been hit with a branding iron. It released its hold on Carl's neck and dropped him to the ground. He landed at the very edge of the chasm and stumbled forward onto his knees.

The beast screamed and swatted at the searing pain in its chest. It clawed at the blade that had pierced its hide by less than an inch, knocking it to the ground, where it fell in front of Carl. The sheriff stared down at the weapon as he fought to regain his breath, unable to retrieve it.

Stephanie released the projectile and let it fly. The musket-sized rock hit the beast in the shoulder, causing an even louder concussion of torment to spew from its lungs. It threw its head backwards, stamped its feet against the floor, and turned in her direction.

She quickly reloaded another magnetic rock into the weapon's pouch and drew back on the bands. The musket ball sailed through the air at her target and missed the creature's head by less than an inch. On the other side of the chasm, Don held the wrist rocket that Troy had given him and attempted to draw a bead on the creature. Don let the projectile sail, missed his mark, and came closer to hitting Carl than connecting with the beast.

Carl struggled to fill his lungs, raking in one shallow breath after the next. The muscles in his throat screamed after almost being crushed by the oppressive strength of the monstrosity. He swayed on the precipice of consciousness, then he felt it, an itch in the base of his skull.

Carl ...

Panic seized him as the horrible voice penetrated his head and spoke. He looked at the dagger laying on the floor in front of him; it had been the only thing protecting him, his only defense against the voice.

Carl ...

It forced its way inside his head, knocking down the barriers he had constructed to hold back the memories of war. It ripped through the façade he had fabricated to convince himself that he was never meant to experience love. And it smashed through his rationalizations that Lois was better off without him.

Carl ...

He stared down at the dusty rock floor of the cavern as his eyes glazed over and the blood vessels ruptured within.

Carl!

The presence invaded him like a virus. Carl arched his back and screamed from the very base of his core, powerful enough to tear his vocal cords down the center. He lowered his head, every muscle in his body rigid and flexed to the point of popping.

Less than twenty feet away, Stephanie watched. She spotted the ancient dagger lying on the floor, just out of the sheriff's reach. She loaded another stone into her weapon and trained her aim on her new target; she focused the bead directly at Carl's head.

The dimness of the void had been altered. Something had changed within, and the change had been sudden. A penetrating illumination now filtered in from the outer edges of the vast emptiness. It transformed the landscape and affected the creature, which now appeared frantic and agitated. The dark transforming mass looked as if it were searching for a way to escape.

Initially, Troy had believed that his strange new surroundings were the domain and the reality of the Ojanox, but now, he wasn't so sure. He was still very much aware and had found a familiar place to hide, but what made him even more certain was his ability to watch the creature from his vantage point without it being able to detect him. *Maybe the Ojanox created this place, but now that I'm here, it's not the only builder.* Troy thought the presence of Scream in the Dark confirmed that.

The dark shadow raced past the cage, directly in front of where Troy stood. The massive cloud of twisting particles shimmered and warped like a school of herring. Its individual atoms were in a perpetual state of motion, each one repelling the other, sending their adjacent brothers into warp speed. It looked as if the beast's body was in a constant state of flux, as if it were attempting to attain wholeness but never able to accomplish the task. *That's why it changes the people into so many different things. Too much information. It can't decide what it wants to become.*

The mass continued its frenetic movements and then rocketed away from Troy's hiding place. He skidded his foot along the floor, comforted that the object was still there. He listened to the sound of his own heart hammering inside his temples and let out an exaggerated sigh.

Troy jumped as something touched his hand. He turned to the left and watched as the outline of the girl slowly took form. Her features were unclear, transparent, and washed in the same iridescent glow as he. Then she took his hand in hers and squeezed it, and Troy knew. Wendy stood beside him within the confines of the cage; she had found her way to him. He held his breath as her outline wavered before him. A moment later, the second figure appeared.

Dawn was there as well. The child looked over at Troy, pressing herself against Wendy as close as she could get. Both girls appeared to understand what he intended to do. Wendy squeezed his hand tighter and wrapped her arm around Dawn. Their voices echoed within his head as clearly as if they had spoken out loud. Although neither had said a word, Troy understood their message. *Don't worry. I'll be ready.* He replied as Wendy released his hand. Troy pressed his foot against the object and placed his hands on the bars.

The Ojanox moved faster than it had before. It darted from place to place, frantically searching the void for a way to escape. Not sure how he had come to possess such knowledge, Troy was certain the creature was just as trapped as they were and had no idea how it had happened. It wasn't used to surprises and wasn't good at thinking on its feet. It was an instinctual creature at best.

The void itself had shrunk to a confining dimension. The Ojanox collided with some invisible barrier and ricocheted backward like an infuriated pinball. Its screams split the static air. They were impossible to bear and made Troy's stomach churn. The beast doubled back and headed toward them once again. Wendy's voice sounded inside his head, and although no words had been spoken, he knew what she said. It was the very thing he had been thinking. The beast sped toward them at a dizzying speed. Troy didn't know if it would work or if he was even strong enough. Fortunately, he didn't have time to second-guess himself as the dark mass descended on him like a storm.

Troy stepped down on the small foot switch he had taped to the floor in his own garage. There was a click, and then there was ... nothing! He heard the death stomp of the switch as it engaged, and the world paused as if it were solidified in time. Hope abandoned him as he realized it had all been for nothing. He had failed, and he had been so sure his plan would work. A half a second later, the strobe light came to life, filling the void with a pulse of searing white light. The beast stopped in front of the cage and screamed. Paralyzed by the blinding light, the Ojanox froze, just inches away from the children. Troy flung his arms outward and plunged them into the distorted mass of particles. He envisioned himself seizing the beast by the throat and clamping down with all his strength.

He clenched his fists together as it squirmed. The creature writhed and bellowed and struggled to free itself. Troy sensed the monster's fear; he could taste its panic, hot and metallic like melting copper. The Ojanox threw itself against the side of the cage to get at him, but Troy held on and closed his eyes. Then ... he felt it ... The cold tightness wrapped around his own throat and clenched down.

The shock was immediate. Paralysis gripped the Entity, and it lost control of all it possessed, including Carl and the one called Butchie. The shock was fleeting, but it was just enough for Carl to regain a sense of where and who he was.

He looked up as Stephanie released her projectile and felt the air break, with the musket ball passing just inches in front of his face. The creature that towered before him appeared to stagnate, but only for a moment. Its body stiffened and tensed, then it focused its attention on the area where the Fischers stood on the other side of the chasm. The Butchie-thing shrieked and lumbered in their direction.

Carl felt the pressure build between his temples as the presence attempted to regain control. He knew once it started speaking, there would be no fighting the voice, that he had maybe a second or two at best. He sprang to his feet, stumbled on the heels of his boots, then lunged at the beast and wrapped his arms around it. He pulled it in tight and struggled to plant his feet. Carl took a step backward.

The great creature howled in shock and lashed out at the man with an exaggerated swat of its arm. It was enough to offer Carl a better hold on it. He pulled with all his strength and hooked his boot heels into the edge of the drop-off. The beast lost its own footing and was set off balance by the sheriff's momentum; it fell onto Carl as he yanked it toward him.

Carl!!!

It screamed within his head as it took him. But it was too late. Carl dug his heels into the rock and pushed backward, sending himself over the cliff. The creature was dragged along with him; they both left the rock and became airborne. Their bodies cartwheeled over one another as they plummeted toward the dark pool below.

Carl felt the presence release control of his mind. Soaring downward, he saw the faces of the men, women, and children who had died on his watch. He was responsible for all of them. He saw Gary Forsyth and David Rainey, the faces of Alice and Will Tobin, and was even offered a vision of Felix Castillo. Bob Jones appeared before him, holding out his hand. They all came to him as Carl plunged faster into the darkness with the beast clutched firmly in his grip. Dr. Malcolm looked over his glasses at him. His face was replaced by Tara Jefferies, whose face was then replaced by Mandy Griggs. Jackie Gilmartin and Abe Gorman were there. Father Kieran nodded and winked. There was another who joined him; Ethan Ziegler offered Carl a satisfied look of approval; Ziegler smiled and then disappeared.

As Carl hit the shallow water, there was only one face he saw and only one person he was left thinking about. He saw Lois, the way she looked the moment before they broke up, her eyes shining and her face unaffected by time. She looked at him and kissed him. *I was finally able to save you,* Carl thought as he hit the water. Both he and the creature were snuffed out like a flame.

CHAPTER 105

"No!" Lois screamed. She took a staggering step closer to the chasm, but Don stopped her. There was nothing either of them could do. She turned and buried her face into the crook of her husband's shoulder.

From across the drop-off, Stephanie watched as the sheriff and beast fell over the edge and disappeared. She could see Don and Lois clearly on the opposite side and had an idea why it had not only grown brighter within the cavern but had gotten warmer as well. There was movement from somewhere in the cave. It bounced off the walls and echoed off the ceiling, making it impossible to discern where it was coming from. Stephanie looked back at the child on the altar, then stared across the chasm to where the other girl lay. Both Wendy and Dawn appeared to be resting and didn't move a muscle. Being as careful as possible, Stephanie crept to the edge of the drop-off and peered over the side.

There was no sign of either the sheriff or the creature; both of their bodies had sunk to the bottom of the strange pool. But now Stephanie understood where the sound was coming from. The water at the bottom of the pit had begun to churn like a whirlpool or a tornado. It swirled in a counterclockwise motion and glowed with the same milky white illumination that it had the first time they saw it. She gasped as the water increased in speed and the lumens intensified. She took several steps back from the edge and the cave erupted with the deafening roar of a hurricane. It sounded as if the air itself were being ripped apart. Stephanie hurried back to the altar where Wendy lay and held on tight to the rock.

On the other side of the pit, Don and Lois jumped as the explosive sound filled the cavern. Troy flung his arms into the air once again and cried out, clawing at something only he could see. Lois tried to reach for him, but Don stopped her just before Troy lashed out at the air where her face would have been. Then the center of the pit exploded like the top of Mt. Vesuvius.

It turned on the boy and seized him. Somehow, the child had managed to hold on to a portion of himself and survive the confines of the domain. But nothing had ever managed such a thing; no creature had ever retained even a glimmer of their individuality after being consumed. It had sensed the boy was different the moment it encountered him. It had known Troy would make a valuable addition to the collective, but it had lost everything in the pursuit of this sole acquisition. It turned on the child with a rage like it had never known. It lashed out and seized Troy by the throat. Looking deeply into the strange child, it found it was still unable to penetrate him completely. It squeezed tighter and shook ... it would shake the very life out of him if need be.

Survival ... it had survived since the beginning of time itself and had only been thwarted once or twice in the past. Which had always been due to its own thirst and hubris. But it had never been stopped by a single child, and it wasn't about to let that happen now. It slammed into Troy, forcing the boy against the bars of his own hiding place. But the child held fast and tightened his own grip as well.

Troy was aware of everything as the creature stared into him and searched through his memories. He felt the beast rifle through his past and insecurities, and felt his own hatred rise within him. The sense of violation was repulsive. Troy detested the feeling and pulled the creature against the bars just as it had done to him. He stared into the dark mass and screamed within the beast's mind in a voice as loud as creation.

The two squared off against one another in an exchange of intimate knowledge. The creature had stolen countless souls over the millennia, but it had never experienced a symbiotic connection like this. It had never assimilated anything that could withstand its intrusion. And Troy, who was only ten and had just recently kissed a girl for the first time, had never imagined a connection on such a profound level.

Troy experienced the creature's entire existence, starting from the moment of its inception. He sifted through the knowledge it had gathered from the countless identities it had consumed in the past. He found himself on the playground, sitting next to his friend, talking about Scream in the Dark. He found himself behind Marco's, stealing cardboard to make their haunted house. And he found himself back in kindergarten, on his very first day of school. He sat next to the boy who would become his best friend and watched as a solitary tear ran down Robert Boyle's cheek. The visions faded, but the shadows were all still there, locked inside the beast. The resonating echoes of Rob and Erin and Ben and all the rest of his friends, waiting to be set free.

Troy screamed and pulled the monster closer. Their combined consciousness attacked itself and one another within the confines of the void, a creation manifested by them both.

Stephanie took Wendy's hand as a tower of light projected from the pit like the beacon of a lighthouse. It shot out of the mouth of the chasm, focusing its concentrated beam on the very center of the cavern's ceiling. The sound that accompanied it caused her ears to pop as it consumed the entire chamber. Her hair whipped across her face as a gale force wind emerged from nowhere. It increased in speed and tore through the cave like a cyclone, casting dust and loose fragments of rock into the air. She hovered over Wendy to protect the child from the flying debris and looked across to notice that Lois had done the same. Don hobbled toward the altar where Dawn lay to defend the child from the swirling particles as well.

The strange milky water that had begun to churn at the bottom of the pit erupted, and a waterspout jettisoned into the air. It cycloned and spiraled, following the tower of light. Together, water, air, and earth combined in a cataclysmic spectacle.

The force of the wind threatened to tear the adults from their positions, causing each of them to cling to the stone altars and onto the children to prevent them from being swept away.

The tornado of water and light lifted out of the mouth of the pit and formed a vortex. It spun counterclockwise as it lifted into the impossible lodestone formation centered in the ceiling of the cave. Now the entire cavern was as bright as a summer day and nearly as hot.

Don threw himself over Dawn to shield her from the raging cyclone and noticed that not all of the light originated from the anomaly in the center of the room. Dawn had begun to emit a light of her own. Staring down at the child, he saw where it was coming from. The medallion she wore glowed as if it had been placed in a kiln. The large stone burned a white-hot golden color; it spread out across the child's chest, filling her face with the aura. It grew brighter and brighter until Don was forced to shield his eyes from the intense glare.

He turned away and looked over at Lois and Troy. A similar brilliance had settled over his son, covering his body almost entirely. The same happened with the medallion that Wendy wore. The dark stone turned red at the center of the sunburst, then spread out to the individual fingers of its crafted sun. The glow intensified, changing from a deep red to a hot white. Then the entire stone lit up as if it were on fire.

Stephanie stared down at the spectacle for as long as she could, until she finally had to look away. She hadn't been sure what to expect when she insisted the children be brought to the cave. There was something at work that no historian or geologist or any other human would ever be able to explain. They were in the presence of something great, something powerful, something that defied explanation. The way the light spread out across the child's chest and then radiated within her face caused Stephanie to think of transformation, of creation ... They were in the presence of something holy.

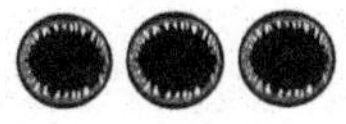

Troy felt the creature struggle within his grasp but sensed his own life force slipping even faster. The beast clamped down on his throat as they faced off, staring into the other's very essence. The stream of consciousness shared between them was more than intimate; it was parasitic. Neither could survive without the other. As Troy exhaled and the monster inhaled, a steady flow of universal information passed between them.

The void came to life, burning with an even brighter light than the steady pulse that the strobe provided. The dark mass whaled itself against the bars, tightening its grip around the child's neck in a last-ditch attempt to consume him. Troy cried out with a thousand blades piercing his skull. Terror raced through the ancient enemy as the light intensified, causing the shadows to recede into the furthest reaches of the void. It panicked and focused every ounce of its energy on destroying the boy, even if that meant its own destruction.

Troy gagged and felt his body go numb. His vision blurred, and his lungs raged like a furnace. He felt his legs begin to give out from underneath him. Then the world erupted in a concentrated beam of white light. It blasted out of the center of Troy's chest and focused on the beast. He watched his hands fight to contain the swirling mass as the light consumed them. The creature bore down on his throat, and Troy slipped away. It tore free from his hands and disappeared into the blinding brilliance of the void as he lost consciousness. The last thing he heard was the wail of the creature as he, too, was silenced. Troy and the Ojanox were consumed by the light.

Lois struggled to protect Troy as he convulsed against the stone altar. With the pendant glowing as if it were on fire, the child thrashed and flailed and struck his mother in the chest. Lois stumbled and moved to return to his side but was unable. She watched as Troy arched his back and screamed like his lungs were being ripped out. A billowing plume of concentrated smoke erupted from the boy like a geyser. It rushed out of him in a flood and was swept away by the brilliant tornado of light. Dark particles shimmered as they emerged from Troy's eyes and nose, then quickly disappeared on the current of air. The flow that was expelled from the child appeared to be endless, and Lois shielded herself by turning away. Then she noticed the other children were in the grips of a similar process. The reflective particles were being ejected from all their bodies.

Seconds later, Troy collapsed against the altar with a thin tendril of smoke lifting from his lips. It was swept away and was gone. Then the swirling cyclone of light and water stopped as if it had been turned off by a switch. The chamber fell silent and began to grow dark once again. Lois looked down at Troy. His head lay tilted to the side; it was impossible to tell if he was breathing or not. She rushed to her son and took him in her arms.

She lifted him from the stone table, and his body hung limp, as if it weighed nothing at all. Then she heard the voice of the young girl, crying and frightened. Wendy coughed and called out as Stephanie took her in her arms. On the other side of the cavern, Don comforted Dawn as she, too, woke from the impossible nightmare. But Troy remained motionless. Lois pressed her cheek to his lips to check his breathing. There was nothing; he was as still as a corpse. Lois shook him and pulled him tight against her chest.

"Troy!" Lois screamed.

His skin looked blue in the fading light. Dark circles spread out beneath his eyes as if he was still wearing his vampire makeup. Lois grabbed his face and pressed her lips over his mouth. *Cold.* Troy Fischer had already started to grow cold in his mother's arms. Lois exhaled into his mouth and prayed. *Please, God, don't let him die. Don't take my son!* She breathed into him once again as the realization slipped like a knife between her ribs and pierced her heart. She had lost him.

"Troy!" she screamed at him. Lois's tears raked through her completely and penetrated her soul.

A rush of air escaped from Troy's mouth. A second later, he began to cough and fought to control his breath.

Lois's tears intensified, though for a much different reason. "Troy!" She leaned him forward and patted him on the back. "Oh, God, thank you. Th-thank you, God."

He raked in the cool air of the cavern one shallow breath at a time until, finally, the coughing fit passed. Troy opened his eyes and looked up at his mother. He tried to speak but was unable and smiled as best he could.

"I thought I lost you, kiddo." Lois continued to cry as she hugged him with all her strength. "Oh, thank God. I don't know what I would have done."

Don lifted Dawn into his arms and felt the ground lurch beneath him. He sensed what was happening and turned toward the small opening in the rock.

"Run!" he screamed. "It's about to cave in."

The entire cavern shook as if a bomb had been dropped on the mountain. Don knew the explosion at the sanatorium could be responsible for the seismic tremors but believed there was another explanation. First the ground heaved as if in the grips of a tectonic shift, and then the ceiling started to give out.

"Now!" he shouted again, but the others were already on the move. Ignoring the pain in his ankle, he carried Dawn in his arms and headed toward the exit. He gritted his teeth and met up with Lois and Troy just as the first boulder-sized stalactites started to rain down from the ceiling.

Stephanie carried Wendy and was the first to step into the second chamber. She sprinted past the ancient murals with the young girl in her arms and stepped out into the twilight of the evening a moment later.

Don and Lois followed with the floor of the cavern pitching and lurching beneath their feet. They exited into the second chamber and were halfway to the mouth of the cave when a rush of dust and debris exploded from the small opening behind them. It blanketed the cavern, making it impossible to see, but they kept moving forward through the murky cloud. They held their breath and closed their eyes. They emerged from the cave just as the roof of the second chamber collapsed. The group retreated from the billow of choking dust and made their way to the center of the quarry.

The tremors lasted for another minute or so before they finally ceased. When the dust lifted and the group was able to see clearly, the entrance to the cave lay blocked by several tons of lodestone and granite. The DuCain site was lost forever, along with everything inside.

CHAPTER 106

A hush fell over the occupants of the truck as Don navigated a safe passage through what remained of Garrett Grove. Troy, Wendy, and Dawn stared out the windows in shell-shocked disbelief. Not a residence or business had been spared, not a soul walked the streets of the once safe neighborhoods, and not a single living creature stirred as the vehicle lumbered through town. What captured the focus of the children even more than the level of destruction was all the discarded Halloween decorations. Smashed jack-o'-lanterns littered the streets; their hollowed-out eyes stared back accusingly as they passed. Plastic skeletons had been ripped from front porches and lay strewn everywhere. The hand-painted murals on the front windows of the businesses had been broken into thousands of tiny pieces.

Doris, Burt, and several of the seniors from Botany Village watched as the first members of the group walked through the side entrance of the medical center. Baxter jumped up to greet them and began to whine the second he saw Dawn being carried in as if she'd been injured. He sniffed the entire group thoroughly, unable to find the man who had saved him, the one called Ted. Baxter let out another whine and followed them to the emergency room.

Stephanie rushed to Janis's bedside and took hold of her hand. Looking down, she noticed the slightest flush of color had returned to her daughter's cheeks. Janis lay motionless for a moment, slowly breathing in and out, then she gently turned her head and spoke. "Mom, is that you?"

"Oh, thank God!" Fresh tears streamed down Stephanie's cheeks, streaking away at the dust that covered her face. "I'm here, baby. It's over; it's finally over. Everything's going to be all right."

Burt held his breath as the rest of the group filed through the door. He waited, hoping the next face he saw would be that of his oldest friend and the man he had thought of as a son. Carl would waltz in wearing his cowboy hat, his face even more weathered from experience rather than age, and he would no doubt have a slick comment waiting on his tongue. Burt watched as Donald Fischer walked in and let the door close behind him. He locked eyes with the man and read volumes. Carl hadn't made it; his friend wasn't coming back.

"He saved us," Don said. "If it wasn't for Carl, none of us would have survived. And that thing would still be out there."

Burt wiped his eyes and nodded. Somehow, he already knew. Call it a premonition or a feeling in his gut, but Burt thought he had sensed the loss of the man right away. He sighed as a hollowness burrowed into his chest. A memory of what Carl had offered to do for him nearly a week ago crept up. He had been willing to risk his job to help Burt because that's the kind of guy Carl Primrose was. He had become Garrett Grove's sheriff because he wanted to help people. And that's exactly what he had done. *Not a bad way to go, my friend.* Burt wiped his eyes again and realized he had been wrong about one thing. As it turned out, there was quite a bit of dignity found in death after all ... quite a bit. He shook his head and gazed down at the state of the children. "Let's have a look at them, shall we?"

Troy, Wendy, and Dawn were rushed into the emergency room and placed in beds not far from where Janis lay talking to her mother. Burt and Doris examined and washed the dirt from the children's faces, checked their vital signs, and diagnosed them no worse for wear.

Troy lay back against the pillow and closed his eyes for a moment. A wave of exhaustion crashed against him like a storm. The child's eyelids appeared too heavy to fully open, even when his father called his name.

"Troy ... are you all right, kiddo?"

He cracked open his eyes and stared at his parents through the parted slits.

"Did we get them, Dad?" he asked.

"Yeah, kiddo. We got them."

Troy opened his eyes fully and looked up at his parents.

Lois gasped and lifted her hand to her mouth. She stared down at Troy in horror. His eyes had always been the same shade as hers, a deep blue the color of the sapphire. But now, something had changed. His right eye was the same as it had always been, but the left one was so dark it almost looked black. Not like the eyes of those who had been infected by the creature, completely blacked out as if by ink. Instead, Troy's iris itself had changed color and was now the shade of rich dark chocolate.

Lois turned to Don, who had noticed it as well. Neither said a word. A lifetime of unspoken resentments once threatened to tear their family apart, none of which now seemed to matter. Troy had been gone, stopped breathing for nearly a minute—they had almost lost him. Time stopped as they looked down at their son, his eyes affected by the unearthly exchange.

Don wrapped his arm around his wife as Lois took Troy's hand in her own. They had somehow survived, and somehow, they were all still together. Few had been so lucky. Troy was alive, and that in itself was a miracle. Possibly it was a sign that they, too, were worthy of a second chance.

Suddenly the curtain behind them swung open, causing them to start.

"Would you keep it down." Billy looked up from the bed. "I'm trying to sleep."

His chest was bandaged, and his face was pale, but he was still kicking; the kid really did have nine lives.

Troy turned to his cousin. "We got 'em, Billy," he said. "Every last scrap."

Billy stared back into his cousin's eyes and froze. His face turned a full shade paler as he focused on Troy's one darkened eye. "I'm not so sure about that, kiddo," Billy said. He laid his head against the pillow and stared up at the ceiling. "I'm not so sure about that at all."

AFTERWORD

Excerpt from the Warren Chronicle

After a mysterious outbreak, the town of Garrett Grove has been placed under quarantine. The unknown contaminant is responsible for numerous cases of infection and countless deaths. The National Guard was dispatched Friday to cordon off the area from neighboring communities. Dr. Devlin from the CDC stated that the contagion has been limited to the small town. The origin of the outbreak is still unknown, and the CDC has not determined whether the outbreak was viral or bacterial.

Several small boats carrying survivors arrived in Butler late Thursday. The crafts' occupants were reported to be raving and delusional with stories of monsters and strange creatures. All of the town's survivors, including those that arrived on the boats, were transported to Walter Reed Army Hospital in Washington and are under quarantine. Major David Werner reports the conditions of the survivors are grave and their survival is unlikely.

The President advises residents in the neighboring areas to stay away from the town of Garrett Grove. The National Guard had been authorized to use extreme force to maintain the quarantine. There is no further information at this time.

Epitaph

The grounds where the old sanatorium once stood were littered with gopher holes. The inhabitants of those burrows had vacated when the dark presence moved into the old hospital. It drove them from their dens far more efficiently than any poison could have ever done. But now, something was stirring once again in one of those forgotten holes.

It pulled itself out of the ground, into the dim glow of the blue moonlight. It shook as a tremor raced throughout its body, causing even more of the animal's fur to fall from its hide. Patches where hair still clung to its flesh grew less and less with each passing minute. Its once ginger-colored coat had been reduced to a matted tangle of dark patches. Its ink-black eyes stared out across the old parking lot.

In another life, it had dined on leftover slices of turkey and hamburger that a young waitress named Mandy had been kind enough to offer. Now it feasted on consciousness and fear. The horrid-looking cat honed in on a lone mole that had lingered on the mountain for far too long. The dark presence leapt from the disfigured animal's mouth and entered the tiny rodent. It wasn't exactly satisfying, but it was a start.

The creature that had once been known as Scraps looked up at the pale moon and shivered once again. Then it darted across the parking lot and set its attention in another direction. Scraps headed north and followed the far side of the mountain ... directly toward the town of Warren.

April 2020 – February 2024

Thank you for reading!

Please consider leaving a rating/review on Goodreads and Amazon.

The Ojanox Series: Books 1 - 4

The Ojanox Series is now available at Amazon and Barnes & Noble.

ACKNOWLEDGEMENTS

If you ever find yourself in the town of Pompton Plains, New Jersey, and drive to the very top of Mountain Avenue, you will reach Mountainside Park, but you won't find an old road extension or an abandoned sanatorium. However, the inspiration for the old hospital comes from a place called the Overbrook, which wasn't all that far away. Neither is the real Garrett Mountain, for that matter. I took great liberties when writing this book, even changing the location to upstate New York, but many of the features are similar to the town I grew up in: Chilton medical center, the graveyard behind the Lutheran Church, even the hardware store at the corner of Jackson Ave. I just changed things a little to fit the story.

It's been four years since I first started writing this book, and there are many who helped bring this monster to life. Whether their assistance was inspirational, fact-checking, information gathering, or emotional support, I couldn't have done this without them. There are topics I touched on in *The Ojanox* that required the input of professionals and tons of research. When it comes to toxicology, lab work, virology, and bacteriology, I did my best to stick to the facts. When I got it wrong—when faced with serving the story or the hard medical facts, I chose the story. So that's on me.

First, I would like to thank Wendy Nastasi and my sister, Dawn Chiossi (Danielle), for a lifetime of inspiration, support, and for listening to me talk about nothing other than this damn book for the past three years. I would also like to thank them for lending their namesakes to this story, with written consent, of course.

There are several friends who read early versions of this book whose help was instrumental. Nick Gomes and Ed Koloski helped provide feedback and were my sounding board from the very start, back in the halfway house days. Greg Gillick and Mike Turrigiano have always had my back and were there to listen to my very first attempts at horror writing. And of course, Jack Wells. Jack has been my constant go-to guy with this project for years. He read it before the first rewrite, and he still came back for more. Now that's a true friend. In truth, *The Ojanox* wouldn't be half the book it is today without Jack's knowledge, skill, and literary prowess.

My editor, Lisa Lee Tone, took every page of this manuscript and made it better with her diligent attention to detail. I'm fortunate to have Lisa in my corner to call me out when I stray from the path, and I'm thankful she was always there to rope me back in.

I'd like to thank Ben Eads for his original developmental edits on *Scream in the Dark* and for the rigorous Jedi training and instruction. (Insert Yoda voice) Because of you, a better writer, I am.

Christy Aldridge has been so much more than a cover artist, or an illustrator, or even a contributor—she has been a partner, in every sense of the word. Without Christy's hard work and dedication, this project wouldn't be half of what it is today. For the past year or more, we have been joined at the hip. She took my vision and brought it to life. Thank you, Christy, I couldn't have done this without you. Now we need to start a new project.

Thank you, Don Noble and Jeff DeSantis for contributing your amazing illustrations and talents to this project.

Many thanks to my Alpha team and proofreaders for their time, input, and suggestions: Donna Latham, Heather Ann Larson, Jae Mazer, Kerrie Roylance, Bryan Moyer, Kristen Lynch, Susan Isenberg, John O'regan, Christina Marie, and Maryanne Pacheco Chappell.

And a huge thank you to Kira (Eagle Eyes) Seamon, for tirelessly hunting through these manuscripts, making sure that all the finishing touches were properly in place. It's the little things that make the difference, and had it been up to me, far too many little things would have slipped through the cracks. Thank you, Kira for squashing all those pesky little things into oblivion.

For all my friends who follow me on social media, for all the reviewers, bloggers, influencers who support the indie horror community, thank you. Also, thank you Tiffany Koplin, RJ Roles, and all the admins at the Books of Horror Facebook group for everything you do.

My life would have been very different if it hadn't been for my fourth-grade teacher, Mrs. Genevieve Smith, whose tutelage, undying devotion, and wealth of limitless stories molded not only myself but an entire generation. I especially would like to thank you for bringing my homework to the hospital when I broke my leg.

Thank you, Kelly Rainey, and all the fourth-grade classes of Pompton Plains school.

Anthony Lorraine helped by sharing with me his experiences in Vietnam. Without Anthony, the character of Carl Primrose would have been much different, as well as my knowledge of that moment in history. Sadly,

I learned of Anthony's passing when I was still in the halfway house. He was a good friend during a dark moment in my life. I miss you, Tony.

Thank you to my family and friends who helped contribute to the inspiration of this story through a lifetime of experiences, which I in turn felt compelled to fictionalize. And finally, for my mom, who told me my first ghost story, took me trick-or-treating, and allowed me to have a Halloween party at the house when I was ten years old. And for my dad, who let me build a haunted house and still reminds me periodically that I painted his garage walls black.

And thank you to the readers and horror fans who love this genre as much as I do. Thank you for taking this journey with me and thank you for allowing me to share this story with you. I hope you enjoyed it half as much as I enjoyed writing it.

Daemon Manx

About the Author

Daemon Manx is an American author with a backstory. He is a recovering addict who spent nearly a decade in the prison system where he focused on recovery and learned to perfect his horror writing craft. He has been featured in magazines in both the U.S., the U.K, and Germany. In 2021 he received a HAG award for his story *The Dead Girl* and was nominated for a Splatterpunk award that same year.

He was a bonus round winner on the gameshow *Wheel of Fortune* in 1999 and is infamously known for a motor vehicle accident he was responsible for, involving President Ronald Reagan's limousine.

After struggling with addiction and incarceration, Daemon now has over eleven years clean and sober. He uses his story to illustrate the positive outcome of sobriety and offer a glimpse at what life can be like when one receives a second chance.

He lives with his sister, author Danielle Manx and their narcoleptic cat, Sydney, where they patiently prepare for the apocalypse. There is a good chance they will run out of coffee far too soon.

Printed in the USA
CPSIA information can be obtained
at www.ICGtesting.com
CBHW020230100924
14064CB00007B/78